Armed and Clueless

G. Daniel

HL

Highline Books

HL

Highline Books

ARMED AND CLUELESS
© 2018 G. Daniel

FIRST EDITION

Library of Congress Control Number: 2018901476

ISBN 978-0-9910281-3-9 softcover (full size)
ISBN 978-0-9910281-4-6 e-book (Kindle)

Highline Books

New York, NY

contact: publisher@highlinebooks.com

Events depicted in this book *will* happen.

1

THE GREAT AMERICAN GUN SHOW

Devoid of good intent, brothers Joseph and Jacob Luntz stand in line, waiting to enter the Great American Gun Show. Since they've both accumulated criminal records for acts such as assault and aggravated menacing, stocking up for their upcoming adventure through legal means is out of the question. This is where the sanctity of the gun show comes into play. Producing identification and answering questions is off-limits. Cash does the talking.

The organizers of this event argue that most of those attending are law-abiding citizens. This may well be the case. However, they like to gloss over the fact that "most customers" doesn't in any way mean *all* customers. They can console themselves with the likelihood most of the victims of the non-law-abiding attendees will be from someone else's family.

Regardless of the typical arguments, the Luntz brothers aren't here today to debate the merits of liberty or firearm laws. They're here to stock up on their toys of choice. The first thing catching their eyes is the row of AR-15 assault rifles. Flush with cash, they scoop up a dozen of these weapons. They can resell some of them to their militia buddies for a tidy profit.

Now stocked with multiple high-capacity clips, along

with hundreds of rounds of ammunition, they next move to a nearby booth. Here, after a brief discussion, the proprietor slips them the simple instructions and bump stock parts for full automatic conversion of these weapons in exchange for another wad of cash. Their methamphetamine sale profits sure can buy a lot of firepower.

Now they have the means, along with a wanton disregard for consequences. The fanatical Luntz brothers are ready to make their stand.

They spend the next two weeks planning and scoping out targets. For dramatic effect, they had at first planned to strike a theater during a crowded Friday night movie premiere. It was a real disappointment when some clown beat them to the punch out in Aurora, Colorado. They would need to settle for something else.

The Welland Mall, a mere twenty miles from their rural home, provides the most attractive of choices. During the holiday season, it should overflow with shoppers. If they strike the food court on a Saturday during lunch hour, they can rack up the highest body count.

Not content with just committing mass slaughter of innocents, Joseph and Jacob Luntz have an overriding motive. They're hoping to use this wondrous event as the opening skirmish in their planned racial holy war. Both are sporting long, bushy beards and will wear facemasks. During the carnage, the plan is to yell Islamic battle cries, which they expect to provide ample impetus for an upcoming attack on Muslims living within our borders. Although the whole idea may appear far-fetched and half-baked, they refuse to let themselves get dissuaded by their excessive degree of fetching and baking.

Despite their fanaticism, Joseph and Jacob have no intention of making this a suicide mission. Their plan will be to escape intact via a waiting car, driven by one of their militia brothers. Their obvious choice is Jeb Hartley, a man whom they've grown up with and who shares their skewed views of civilization. In fact, when told of their plans, he at first insists on joining the gunplay. With much disappointment, he settles for the role of getaway driver.

As the day of the planned attack approaches, Joseph and Jacob can barely contain their excitement. What they don't possess, along with common sense, is even a shred of apprehension. This is an essential element all true sociopaths share: complete lack of fear or remorse, the most effective body armor of all.

On the Saturday morning of the planned attack, the Luntz brothers are awake at dawn, starting the day with their usual P90X workout, getting pumped to the max. An extra one hundred crunches later, Joseph joins Jacob and Jeb for hearty portions of bacon and eggs. They spend the rest of the time loading their ample stock of ammunition clips. These guys are looking to cause major damage.

The three unwise men kneel in prayer to Lord Jesus, oblivious to the fact he was one of their hated Hebrews. Now dispensing with piety, they jump into their car and head for the mall.

Upon reaching their destination, they encounter a packed parking lot. Joseph gets dropped off at the front entrance while the car circles around to the back. As per the plan, he walks through the food court, averting his gaze so as not to make eye contact with potential victims. He slips into a service corridor, propping open an emergency exit. The others sit at the curb in wait. He jumps into the car and dons a full camouflage outfit, identical to that worn by his brother. Both men pull on their masks, grab their weapons, and share an obligatory fist bump. It's go time.

Seconds later, they encounter their first obstacle. While they've been getting prepared, a security guard has discovered the propped door. Without bothering to look outside, he pulls it shut, thus depriving them of their special access to the mall. Despite the recent development, the brothers are so pumped with adrenaline at this point they refuse to scuttle the mission. Rather than sneak through the rear exit, they instead march right through the main mall entrance in full combat gear.

To their surprise, during the well-armed trek, they're able to avoid scrutiny. Most of the shoppers stay glued to their cell phones, no doubt in the middle of important communications. A security guard could owe his life to the shapely blond shopper who has attracted his undivided attention. The two soldiers of misfortune march right past him, carrying machine guns and wearing full body armor. They stride uninterrupted to their planned positions on opposite sides of the food court. Despite the large crowd, no one gives the brothers a second look.

As they nod to each other, Joseph decides to announce their presence. He jumps up on a table in the middle of the diners, pointing his loaded assault rifle straight toward the ceiling. He shouts his best attempt at the Muslim battle cry "Allahu akbar!"

As the people around him are busy stuffing their faces, no one seems to notice. Frustrated, he reverts to using a good old-fashioned American "Hey!" As he does this, he pulls the trigger, sending a burst of fire into the roof, resulting in a downpour of acoustical tile upon his head. At least he's finally caught people's attention. The falling debris knocks Joseph off balance, causing him to drop his assault rifle while stumbling off the table.

As this is modern-day America, several others in the

food court also bear arms. A portly, middle-aged gentleman is the first to draw his weapon. He shoots in the general direction of where Joseph had been standing. He misses Joseph, who by now has fallen to the floor. The man continues to fire away, even though his target has disappeared, having taken refuge under the table. Subsequent rounds tear into those unfortunate to be sitting in the way.

Next, an elderly woman pulls a revolver out of her purse and fires at the portly gentleman, assuming him to be the original source of the gunfire. Soon, several people at various points around the room have pulled out their handguns and are shooting at one another. There is utter confusion, as none of those firing their weapons can tell the good guys from the bad guys. Anyone holding a drawn gun at this moment has become fair game. Once the pandemonium lets loose, those who aren't bearing arms are in the safest position. The dining area has devolved into a massive, frenzied, free-fire zone. Hungry shoppers are now being exposed to something even deadlier than the fast food.

During the melee, Joseph has been scampering underneath one table after another. Meanwhile, Jacob stands frozen in place while witnessing this madness. He never fires a shot. Instead, he dumps his mask and gun into a waste receptacle. His brother crawls out from under a nearby table, having also ditched his mask and weapon. The two bolt out of the front entrance, melding into the fleeing crowd. After several minutes of random, terrified gunfire by confused, law-abiding citizens, the food court is littered with bodies.

As the Luntz brothers walk around to the rear parking lot, Jeb waits in the driver seat. He has been expecting a dramatic exit, replete with squealing tires and high-speed police pursuit. Instead, the two casually get into the car while telling him he can take his time pulling out. Meanwhile, shots are still ringing out from inside the mall.

Jeb remains excited. He's also confused to see the brothers returning while sounds of the gunfight continue. "So, what happened? From out here, it sounded like you guys were taking Hamburger Hill!"

Joseph is first to speak. "Not quite. I might have kicked over a few hamburgers, but I didn't get to shoot anybody."

He looks disappointed, as does Jeb. Jacob just sits in the back, speechless.

They drive home in stony silence, totally guilty, but legally innocent of mass homicide. Meanwhile, back at the mall, eleven law-abiding citizens have fallen. Each one still grips a handgun with their cold, dead hands. All have an official concealed-carry permit inside their wallets and purses. Our forefathers would be proud.

When the three reach the Luntz home, they turn on the TV, looking forward to seeing coverage of their little adventure. Somewhat disappointed that the mission didn't go as planned and that the body count was only eleven, they still consider it to be an overall success. The broadcast is interrupted by reports of killings at an office park in Houston, along with the murder of a policeman at a traffic stop. Two days later, the media turns its full attention to an elementary school shooting in Newtown, Connecticut. The death toll of first graders has eclipsed that of the shopping mall.

To see their handiwork knocked right off the network news in favor of someone else's endeavors brings them great disappointment. Their murderous achievement has fallen prey to America's ever-shortening attention span.

Joseph snaps, "Turn this shit off."

Jacob grabs the remote, switching over to the video game that's already hooked up to the TV. The brothers spend the rest of the afternoon playing *Call of Duty 2*.

2

THE FRUITCAKE MARKETING PLAN

After the mall and school shootings, the airwaves are crackling with intensity. It's almost enough to knock news of the latest Lindsay Lohan arrest off the air. Almost.

The predictable hue and cry lasts around as long as a *Three Stooges* short, albeit with even more moronic content. At least the Stooges are supposed to be ridiculous.

As expected, the gun lobby proceeds to march out their attack dogs, unleashing them on every cable news network.

Politicians everywhere are ducking for cover. Many stare blankly at TV cameras, reciting the profound concept that the only way to protect ourselves from all the guns out there is with more guns. This is like drilling holes in a sinking boat to let the water out. That idea also came from a Stooges short.

Let the payoffs begin.

Oklahoma Congressman Lenny Homer has become a ubiquitous presence on the cable news networks. They never feature him for having something useful to say, but because his comments are too absurd to come from a grown human being. This qualifies him for limitless broadcast time, as broadcasting devotes itself to those creating the greatest spectacle. Today, he's on TV blaming all gun violence on those dreaded "gun-free" zones.

"They always want to blame all this gun violence on guns, damn it! These shootings have nothing to do with guns. It always involves someone who's mentally ill. If we lock up everyone with mental problems, we can get to keep all our guns."

In a saner society, Congressman Homer would be the first one locked up. Instead, the voters of his district reward these idiotic statements by reelecting him. Maybe they should lock up the whole district.

3

ARMSTRONG FIREARMS COMPANY

The Armstrong Firearms Company sits in a nondescript warehouse in an industrial park outside of Richmond, Virginia. Business has been brisk. However, that isn't good enough for the greedy bastards who run the company.

The executive committee gathers in the boardroom, a well-appointed suite walled in solid cherry. The president of the firm, John Rumsen, sits at the head of a long table, joined by a group of eight corporate officers. He opens the meeting.

"This backlash we're getting from the public has the potential to reduce our profits. If only that fucking fruitcake in Newtown didn't blow away a bunch of six-year-olds. You know, at least at Columbine the victims were high school kids. Since lots of people hate them anyway, it wasn't such a big deal. Now, as fast as we can put guns on the street, those damn bleeding-heart liberals try to take them off. Hell, these assault rifles are our biggest moneymakers. The damn gun-control bastards will cut into our bottom line if we don't strike back. I wish someone would shoot some of *them* instead next time."

The company vice president, Larry Sherman, gives him a reassuring smile.

"I'm sure we can weather the storm, John. You know how these things always go. Whenever a bunch of innocent people get shot, the public makes a lot of noise for a day or two, then they move on to the next outrage. We'll ride this one out, too. You'll see."

Rumsen wants to believe him, but has other concerns.

"I'm sure you're right, Larry. I'm just hoping it doesn't cut into our efforts through our network of lobbyists to make this 'stand your ground' thing into a federal law. This could turn into a real moneymaker for us. The more people find out they can shoot somebody and walk, the more hardware we can expect to sell. However, we only own around half the state legislatures at this point. If this damn school shooting in Connecticut causes too much backlash, we may end up facing more resistance in the remaining states. We might lose out on some big profits."

The company secretary, Luke Velsey, puts in his two cents. "All we need to do is stick with our regular game plan. We'll continue to frame every single attempt at firearm regulation as an assault on the Second Amendment. That line always shuts up our critics."

"Screw the Second Amendment," Rumsen snaps. "I don't care about the right to bear arms, just the right to make money!"

"Look, John, all we need to do is wait it out," Larry says. "The next time there's a mass workplace shooting or some guy takes out a bunch of shoppers at a mall, we'll be back in business. Whenever this stuff happens, we end up making more sales. Nobody has the guts to stand up to us. I wouldn't worry about it. We've become the most protected industry on the planet. Thanks to our bitches in Congress, nobody can sue us anymore. We could even pass out guns to children on their way to school. We're untouchable!"

They all nod in smug satisfaction. Larry continues laying out their plans. "Our associates are also pushing statehouses across the country to open college campuses to firearms. Once a few students get shot, everybody on campus will want a gun. It'll be awesome. I say now's the time to begin a marketing campaign targeting collegians. The accessories market should be huge, too. We'll come out with bulletproof backpacks, Kevlar vests made in the school colors with the university logo on the front. We need to jump on the fast track licensing this stuff."

Luke points out where this push can lead. "After that, public schools should follow. Once we're able to pass a federal law allowing unrestricted concealed carry for all those eighteen and over, we'll make a fortune off high school seniors. The sky's the limit!"

Larry adds, "Someday, every kid will tote a cell phone, a laptop, and a gun. Bullying will be relegated to the past. On second thought, bullies should be our best customers. Is this a great country or what?"

4

MARVIN ROGERS

The Rogers family lives in a gated, upscale community just outside of Orlando, Florida. Emmanuel Rogers, the head of the household, is a well-regarded vascular surgeon. His wife, Tina, who holds a doctorate in psychology, runs a thriving practice. They have three sons.

Their eldest, Marvin, is a star player on the high school basketball team. Gifted in this sport, he's made varsity as a mere freshman. Major universities have taken note, the expectation being he will end up going to college on a full scholarship. Also, as an honor student, Marvin has made his parents most proud.

Bob Cooper lives in the same neighborhood. His life has been one of far greater mediocrity than Marvin's. The only thing that has given him any sense of importance is his concealed-carry permit. Being strapped to a gun gives him more confidence. He even spends his time daydreaming about some situation where he and his pistol save the day. He thus becomes a hero and gets that elusive, awestruck girl.

Due to liability issues, the community in which Bob lives has foregone establishment of a formal neighborhood watch. He decides on his own to anoint himself as head of this nonexistent entity. Besides, an official association would forbid carrying of firearms. As a self-appointed lawman, he needn't follow such rules. What's the point of having a concealed-carry permit if he can't use it?

Since Bob has difficulty maintaining any useful pursuits, he has plenty of time to cruise the neighborhood, keeping an eye out for suspicious characters, especially those with dark skin. He's already called 911 too many times to count, and the police have become weary of him, relegating him to crank status. However, they must follow up on every contact, always finding nothing aside from Mr. Cooper's lack of credibility.

Tonight, Bob foregoes the phone call as he spots a tall, lanky black kid walking down the sidewalk. By sidestepping a call to 911, he can avoid the typical instruction to wait until the police arrive. This will give him greater freedom to take matters into his own hands.

That lanky black kid is Marvin, who is on his way home from basketball practice. At first, he doesn't even spot the dark SUV cruising by in the opposite direction. After the vehicle makes a U-turn and follows beside him, he feels a chill run up his spine. He picks up the pace.

From behind the wheel, Bob decides he doesn't like the looks of this kid. At least, he hopes the kid is up to no good, which will then give him an opportunity to play hero. As he parks the car, he even mutters to himself, "I'm going in."

He jumps out of the ride and is right on the heels of Marvin, who senses an imminent threat.

Bob calls out, "Hey, what the fuck are you doing here?"

Marvin stops and turns. "I'm on my way home. Why are you following me?"

"I've never seen you around here before. I think you're lying."

"I'm not. Why are you hassling me?"

"I'm the neighborhood watch."

"Yeah? Then watch this." With that, Marvin turns and walks toward home.

As his prey moves on, Bob refuses to let it go. He runs to catch up, now standing only a few feet away.

"Hey, boy, I'm talking to you! How'd you like me to plant your black ass in the ground?"

These words, and Bob's proximity, unleash a mix of fear, anger, and adrenaline in Marvin. Forced to stand his ground, he wheels around, punching Bob right in the jaw. Bob cries out in pain as he stumbles backward, falling to the ground.

He jumps to his feet, drawing his gun. Marvin puts his hands in the air, holding nothing more than a cell phone. Now petrified, his voice shaking with fear, he tries to talk his way out of the situation.

"I don't want any trouble. Please let me go home."

A wave of frustration hits Bob, who realizes he can't restrain or arrest this guy. Therefore, he resorts to what he perceives in his own mind to be the only available option. He pulls the trigger.

The last thing Marvin sees is some dope standing over him, gun in hand, realizing he has just taken an innocent human life.

Now Bob gets to be famous. A legion of right-wing talk-radio hosts will soon portray his feeble, misguided attempt at heroics as extreme gallantry. The so-called conservatives will lionize him as a symbol of Second Amendment greatness.

Dead men tell no tales. Meanwhile, the folks who shoot them get to spew some real whoppers.

5

MACK LAWSON

Bob Cooper, looking dapper in his new orange jumpsuit, now sits in the jailhouse meeting room across from his lawyer, Mack Lawson. Mack is the take-charge type. Like many in his profession, he is also the type to take charge of his client's bank account. He skips the small talk, getting right to business.

"You're the neighborhood watch captain, correct?"

"Yep."

"So in that capacity, your neighbors count on you for their safety, right?"

"Yes, sir."

"Tell me what happened the night of the shooting, to the best of your recollection."

"I was coming from the store, scoping things out. You know, keeping an eye on things. I saw this dude walking along, and he didn't look right."

"What about him wasn't right?"

"I don't know. It's an intuition kind of thing. There are drug dealers and thieves prowling around."

"Is there a lot of that activity in your neighborhood?"

"No, not in my neighborhood, but I've seen a lot of it on TV."

"So you thought this guy was out there dealing drugs?"

"No, but you never know. He might have been."

"OK. Where were you when you spotted him? Were you in your vehicle?"

"Right."

"The police report says you didn't call 911. Is that true?"

"Yes, sir, that's correct."

"Isn't it protocol for the neighborhood watch to dial 911 if they encounter something suspicious?"

Now Bob repeats the same lie to his attorney he told the cops.

"I decided I needed to get a closer look before I made the call. It was dark out, and I wanted to make sure I gave them a proper description of this guy. I thought the battery in my cell phone might be low, too."

"Did you plan to wait until you spotted a possible crime in progress?"

"No. Since when do I need to wait for a crime?"

Mack puts his probable-cause lecture on hold, not bothering to waste it on his half-witted client. "So rather than call the police, why did you continue to pursue him?"

"Um, I figured this guy could have stolen something before the cops showed up. Maybe he could have even killed somebody. I couldn't take that chance."

"You sensed someone might be in imminent danger?"

"That's right. These days, who knows what might happen? There are lots of dudes walking around with guns."

"Do you walk around with guns?"

"Yeah, but that's beside the point. I'm the good guy."

Mack is sure everyone sees himself as the good guy. "As watch captain, your charge is to protect the people of the neighborhood?"

"That's right. I'm responsible for whatever happens."

"If anyone got hurt while you sat there and did nothing, you'd be committing dereliction of duty?"

"Um, yeah. I guess I would, come to think of it."

"So you perceived you had the legal responsibility not to let this suspicious character out of your sight."

"That's right."

"You figured it was necessary to leave your vehicle to protect your neighbors from an imminent threat?"

"Yes."

"So you approached the subject?"

"Yeah."

"What did you say to him?"

"I said, 'Hey, what's up?'"

"Did the suspect respond?"

"He told me to fuck off."

"Just like that?"

"Yeah. Just like that."

"Did you say anything back to him?"

"No."

"You said nothing at all?"

"No. Nothing."

Mack believes this must be a crock. He presses the point. "Are you positive you said nothing back to him?"

"That's what I said."

"OK. This is an important point. The police haven't shown me all the evidence. If you say one thing, and someone comes forward and tells them something else, there might be a problem."

"I didn't see any witnesses."

"That doesn't mean there weren't any. Make sure you tell me exactly what transpired. I want you to recount what was said and what was done."

"I will."

"So, this guy told you to fuck off, and you didn't respond?"

"Like I said."

Despite being frustrated at his client's obvious attempt to shade the truth, Mack moves on. "OK. What happened next?"

"He turns around and punches me in the face."

"Did you hit him back?"

"No. I fell to the ground."

"Then what did he do?"

"He stood over me and appeared to reach for a weapon. So I drew my gun, and I fired it."

"According to the police, he was reaching for a cell phone. He died with it in his hand, trying to call 911 for help."

Bob snaps, "Hey! How was I supposed to know what he's holding? Do I need to wait and find out?"

Mack decides not to answer him. "So you feared for your life?"

"Yes. Wouldn't you?"

"I understand. You felt you were in imminent danger."

"I know my rights. The 'stand your ground' law says I can use any means to defend myself. Right?"

"The police say you shot an unarmed man. It would help our case if he'd been reaching for a gun instead of a cell phone."

Now Bob is getting angry and defiant. "Like I already said, I wasn't going to wait and see what he would pull out! OK?"

"Well, you said it at least looked like he was holding a weapon, right?

"That's right, damn it. I'd rather be judged by twelve than carried by six."

Mack would prefer twelve not judge his client, either.

"So you were exercising your rights under the 'stand your ground' law."

"Um, yeah. I know the law, and I know my rights."

"Good. I don't want to get your hopes too high, but I think we're in a pretty strong position here."

"So what happens now?"

"We'll move to have the charges dismissed. You're an innocent guy who was forced to stand his ground."

Bob adopts his best Dirty Harry swagger. "Yeah, you've got it. Maybe the next time one of these punks goes out for a walk, they'll cut through somebody else's neighborhood."

Mack frowns at his client who, thanks to an appalling sense of self-righteousness, has apparently learned nothing from this incident. They used to say clothes make the man. Now it's all about what's in the holster.

6

TED HUNTER

One thing of which there's no shortage is the endless parade of right-wing clowns hosting talk-radio shows. We can thank industry deregulation for this, which a Republican Congress hustled through in 1996. Party operatives coordinated this move and were ready and waiting to snatch up as many broadcasting properties as they could. Now there's no getting away from wall-to-wall political shills hiding behind the microphone. One such shill is Ted Hunter.

He's hosting his daily, coast-to-coast talk show and is pushing all things conservative. This means adopting the uncompromising position that anyone should be able to carry any kind of weaponry anywhere. They expect the rest of us to sit by and shut up. Whether our forefathers had intended to hold the public hostage or not, that has become the prevalent belief.

Ted perches in his favorite hiding place, which is behind a microphone. The station announcer starts the broadcast.

"You're listening to WIMP. Now, it's time to stand up and salute, America! Here's your number one patriot, Ted Hunter!"

The host is ready with the windup.

"Ted Hunter here. Welcome back to the 'Supremacy in Broadcasting' network. I'm having more fun than any human being has a right to. Today, we're talking about the Marvin Rogers shooting in Florida. The lines are lit up, so all you callers out there, please be patient. I'm sure you all want to weigh in. It's obvious the liberals are up in arms over this. They have a problem whenever some patriotic citizen exercises his or her God-given right to self-defense. What do they expect us to do when confronted by a criminal, use harsh language?"

That was a clever line the first time it was used fifty years ago. It has lost some of its luster after being repeated, ad nauseam, by those too clever by one-half. Of course, "too clever by one-half" has also worn out its welcome in the lexicon of less-than-clever clichés. In radio, no cliché goes unturned.

"Mike from Seattle, you're on the air."

"Yeah, Ted. Thanks for taking my call. I also want to say you are a great American."

"Thank you, Mike. That's kind of you."

"Your call screener told me what to say."

A red-faced Ted tries to ignore that comment as he glares at his screener through the studio window.

"Well, moving right along, what's your take on the Rogers shooting, Mike?"

"I'll tell you what. These guys, especially the younger ones, shouldn't walk around dressed like gangsters, for starters. They shouldn't be wearing these hoodies or sports jerseys. They're just asking for trouble. That's all I have to say."

"I agree. If you're not a criminal, you shouldn't be dressing like one. As they say, clothes make the man."

He switches callers. "Bill from Omaha, you're on the air."

"Yeah, Ted. Look, this neighborhood watchman was just doing his job. He has the same right to walk down the sidewalk as anyone else without someone attacking him. This

Rogers punk jumped him for no reason, and he has the right to defend himself. I don't care what these liberals are whining about. I guess they never heard of the Second Amendment. That kid got what he deserved."

"Thank you. Larry from Pittsburgh, you're on the air."

"Hi, Ted, this is Larry. Look, I've been listening to one caller after another blast away at the victim. Sure, that's easy to do. He can't speak for himself—"

As he senses someone may dare not agree with him, Ted interrupts. "Oh, so you'll speak for him? How do you know what happened? Were you a witness?"

"I wasn't there, and neither were you. I don't know all the facts, which also goes for you or any of your callers."

Ted now adopts his usual mocking tone, reserved for those who refuse to drink the right-wing Kool-Aid he serves up daily.

"So get to your point. Or was that it?"

"No. You seem to feel like it's fine for this so-called neighborhood watchman to stand his ground. Well, how about the victim? Isn't he also allowed to stand *his* ground? Is it only the guy with the gun who's allowed to stand his ground? Whose ground is it, anyway? I mean—"

Ted cuts off the caller. "OK. That's enough of your liberal nonsense."

He upbraids his call screener live on the air. "Hey Smedley, aren't you supposed to be screening out these left-wing callers? I will not let them use this show to push their Socialist agenda. Next up is Bob from Wichita. Hello, Bob, and welcome to the 'supremacy in broadcasting' network."

"Hi, Ted. This is Bob. Yeah, I just wanted to say, I hope your last caller gets mugged on the way home. See how he likes it." He hangs up.

As is typical, Ted and his listeners allow little room for

respectful differences of opinion. Besides, respect for others makes for bad ratings. His audience would fit right in at the Coliseum, where they'd be screaming for Caesar to give the thumbs-down. The performance comes to a close.

"That's all we have time for today. As I'm sure you'll all agree, this has been a very informative day. Once again, the leftists out there are trying to take away our guns. We can't allow that. Let me leave you with this: I'd like each one of you to show you're a good, patriotic American by going out, finding a criminal, and shooting him."

7

RANDY STEELE

Randy Steele raises his M4 assault rifle, taking aim. The prey: two 15-year-old Iraqi boys who are kicking a soccer ball back and forth, oblivious to the helmeted, flak-jacketed soldier standing thirty yards away. From this distance, they are dead meat. To him, they are just objects he can use for target practice.

He spent his youth shooting lots of things, living or otherwise. His father gave him a hunting rifle when he was fourteen. What he didn't give Randy was any guidance, discipline, or supervision. Therefore, the bad attitude he gained early in life could manifest itself unchecked. Another kid with a bad attitude, a hunting rifle, and no respect for life was thrust upon the world.

One day, this cold-blooded kid grew up to become a cold-blooded adult. After various stints in jail for making threats, committing assaults, and destroying property, Randy has found an outlet for which he is well suited: the army. Now he can shoot other human beings and get away with it. He sees himself as the perfect killing machine, devoid of feelings. In fact, he has enjoyed it so much that the other soldiers in his unit have grown wary of him. Ever prone to fly off the handle at the slightest provocation, they believe he's even more of a threat to them than a fundamentalist suicide bomber. At least a suicide bomber has semi-tangible excuses for his actions.

The army had intended to weed out people like Randy. It was obvious he was unfit for combat. However, standards were shifted to fill large quotas. With two wars to fight at the same time, the United States is now counting on an all-volunteer force and can ill afford to turn anyone away. Worse still, after being trained to kill with efficiency, these same marginal personalities get sent right back into society after a couple of tours, armed and dangerous.

For Randy, future American civilian targets will just need to wait their turn. In the meantime, he'll settle for two Iraqi boys kicking a soccer ball. He pulls the trigger, emptying the entire mag with a look of pure, vacant joy. This is way more fun for him than playing a combat video game. However, his actions haven't gone unnoticed by another member of his team, who has watched the whole scene unfold, frozen in horror. A few village elders also witness the carnage.

The commanding officer calls Randy in the following day. He knows what the meeting is about, and has prepared how he will respond when confronted. It's the standard, expected response.

"Well, sir, we were out on patrol when our platoon came under fire."

His commander isn't moved. "The soldiers in your unit claim they heard no gunfire, other than your own, that is."

Randy is adamant. He sticks to the number one rule advised of all when facing a similar circumstance: deny, deny, deny.

"That's not true! They were in no position to make the call. I rounded the corner first. It was me against the enemy. Besides, you know how some of the guys in my unit have got it in for me. Why should you take their word for it?"

G. Daniel

They're not alone. The commanding officer has had it in for him, too. Loose cannons find a way of getting the wrong people killed.

"According to witnesses from the village, there was no gunfire. You shot a group of helpless, unarmed kids."

Randy plays it up to the hilt. "Look, man, this is war! Who are you gonna trust, me or a bunch of rag heads? Any of those punks could carry a grenade. I don't need to be taking any chances!"

Now the blood of the commanding officer is also at full boil. "Don't you ever address me as 'man'! Do you understand that? I won't put up with any insubordination, especially from you!"

Randy decides to take it down a notch. "Sorry, sir. I'm telling the truth, and I'll be damned if I'm gonna let myself get blamed by a bunch of these Iraqi cockroaches. You know how much they hate us. They'll say anything."

"It wasn't just the villagers. There was also another man in your unit who saw you open fire. He now conveniently claims he may have been mistaken. I wonder where his sudden case of amnesia came from. You didn't threaten him, did you?"

Of course Randy threatened him. He threatens everybody.

"I don't know what you're talking about."

"The hell you don't. Lucky for you, he's got your back. If we weren't short personnel, I'd have both of you face a court martial."

Randy chuckles to himself at that. He's already had a word with Gary, who saw the whole incident. If there's one thing Randy excels at, it's intimidation. He's a large guy, and the rest of his unit fears him. Behind his back, they refer to him as "Psycho." They'd love to see him disappear, by any means.

Although he dodged the proverbial bullet on this occasion, his propensity for insubordination will eventually earn him a dishonorable discharge. He will thus transport his anger, inconsideration, and utter contempt for others back home to the United States, where he'll fit right in. How lucky for the rest of us.

One of those unfortunate others is Randy's wife, Nancy. Married six months prior to his deployment in Iraq, she was only too glad to see him go. Their marriage up to this point had been two weeks of wedded bliss, followed by five and a half months of utter agony.

It's true she has always found this kind of guy attractive. They've all somehow reminded her of her father. Women such as her can be drawn to men who rule through domination and intimidation. They find a perverse attraction to living under the constant threat of violence. They grow up ill-disposed to being treated with any respect, feeling unworthy of it. If you see yourself as worthless, what does that say about someone who's attracted to you? As a result, guys such as Randy tend to take up with girls such as Nancy, who swear they're only one bruised lip away from leaving. Unfortunately, they rarely do so, until that becomes the least of their problems.

While stationed in Iraq, she prayed he would wind up on the receiving end of an IED. Cursed as she is, he has returned intact. Apparently tending to other matters, God has decided not to honor her request.

8

DATE NIGHT WITH THE STEELES

A late-model car weaves through city traffic just after the dinner hour. Randy Steele is behind the wheel. Nancy sits beside him. They are riding in silence, and there is a visible uptightness between them, meaning nothing is out of the ordinary. He appears to have a permanent scowl etched on his face, what you'd expect from someone who wears his ever-present anger with pride. It is this shield of intimidation he shows toward the world, one which he is unhappy to be a part of.

Up ahead, a traffic light turns from yellow to red. Randy, who has been cruising a good fifteen miles-per-hour over the speed limit, doesn't stop for the signal. Instead of hitting the brakes, he hits the gas, speeding through the intersection well after the light has turned.

Patrolman Charles Morrison is tired, looking forward to the end of his shift after a long day. He's not in the mood to be making any more traffic stops this evening. He sits at a stoplight, waiting for it to turn green. When it turns, he steps on the gas. As he does so, a vehicle flies through the intersection, crashing the red light. Charles needs to slam on his brakes to avoid a collision.

Randy is the one speeding by. He sees the police cruiser in his rearview mirror. The patrol car follows him for several more blocks, while Randy doesn't even bother to slow down. The policeman moves right behind him, and the flashers are lit up.

Upon seeing this, Randy cusses up a storm. Nancy admonishes him, "I told you not to speed."

He snaps back, "Shut the fuck up!"

He pulls to the curb. Charles parks the police cruiser, warily stepping out. He approaches the Steeles' car, rapping on the driver's window. After pausing for a long moment, Randy lowers the window part way.

Charles asks, "Do you know why I pulled you over?"

"No. Why don't you tell me, Your Highness?"

The officer knows he has found some guy with an attitude, which is something he's not in the mood for. "You ran a red light, smart ass."

"Come on! I was about a half a second late. What's the big deal?"

"Your license and registration, please."

Taking his time, Randy pulls out his wallet. "Here's my license. I can't find the registration."

Nancy chimes in, "I think it's at home."

Randy snaps again, "I told you to shut the fuck up!"

Charles tells them, "Wait here." He walks back to the patrol car.

Randy is grumbling the whole time. "I don't like this guy."

"He's just doing his job."

As usual, she says the wrong thing. To Randy, that's whatever comes out of her mouth. Thus, he explodes. "Well, fuck him, and fuck his goddamn job! And if I hear one more fucking word out of you…" As he says this, Randy raises his hand in a threatening way toward his wife.

Charles is on the radio, eyeing the driver with suspicion. Something feels wrong. Guys like this are his least favorite kind of traffic stop. They always want to start a fight. After an indeterminate wait, he receives information on Randy's driving record. Things don't look good. Worried about possible trouble, he calls for backup. As his shift is close to running into overtime, his patience is also running into overtime. Rather than follow protocol, which would mean waiting for another unit, he moves forward with the procedure. Hanging up the mic, he opens his door and walks toward the Steeles' car. He once again taps on the glass, expecting to be the target of further belligerence. Again, Randy takes his time lowering window.

"Sir, did you know you had a court date last month for a speeding ticket?"

"I'll take care of it."

"There's a warrant for your arrest. I need you to step out of the car."

"I said I'll take care of it!"

"Step out of the car, *now.*"

"Hey! What the fuck's your problem?"

Charles is now moving one hand toward his holster, the other toward the door handle. "Sir, step out of the car. I will not ask you again."

"Fuck you!"

As he says this, Charles reaches for the holster while yanking the door open. Randy draws a gun and shoots the officer in the head.

A police backup unit pulls up right as this takes place. Randy makes no attempt to flee. Officers surround him, guns drawn. A policeman barks, "Show me your hands!"

9

LEWIS DARBY

Lewis Darby has earned a reputation for being the top criminal defense lawyer around. He's the first choice in the most extreme circumstances. If somebody were to gun down the mayor in broad daylight on the steps of City Hall, Lewis is the one he would call. He could convince a jury that the mayor had committed suicide.

Caught mowing down a police officer while being videotaped by a dash cam would be an equivalent scenario. In fact, someone would expect to get more sympathy if they had gunned down the mayor instead. Randy figures Lewis is the one to hire, even if it might wipe out his life savings.

Their first encounter is in a jailhouse meeting room. The accused enters wearing a bright-orange prisoner jumpsuit. Lewis looks the more immaculate of the two in his twelve-hundred-dollar threads. After exchanging stilted pleasantries, Randy cuts to the chase. "When do I get out of here?"

This show of audacity puts off Lewis, which is surprising, given his line of work. "Well, Mr. Steele, that depends on how we present this case to the court. Since you shot a cop, it would be a minor miracle just to receive bail."

Randy protests, "It was self-defense! He was drawing his weapon!"

Thanks to that belligerent tone, Lewis can see he may

have an out-of-control client on his hands. Obviously, a lack of control by his clients accounts for most of Lewis's business. Still, he's never comfortable when having to represent a potential loose cannon such as Randy. He knows he must take charge of the situation.

"Settle down. When you get in front of the judge, you will want to be on your best behavior. From what I see, your best might not cut it."

"I'll behave. OK?"

"Don't do so on my account. *Your* ass is on the line. You need to act as if your future is at stake, which it is. Now tell me what happened."

"I got pulled over by this cop. He had this attitude. He was making me nervous. When he ordered me out of the car, I didn't feel like getting out. You know, maybe he might use excessive force."

"What did he say?"

"He told me to get out. I didn't care for the way he said it, so I stayed inside. When he reached for his weapon, I got scared and fired in self-defense."

Lewis sizes up his client for a moment. Although this would seem an impossible case to the average jailhouse lawyer, he relishes the chance to take on the most challenging situations. Spotting a possible line of attack, he asks, "You're a vet, right?

"Yep. Two tours in Iraq."

"You've been taught to react when someone pulls out a weapon, correct?"

"You got it."

"That's good. We can use that. Mr. Steele, have you been having any other difficulties since you've come back from the war?"

"What do you mean by difficulties?"

"I mean, have you had a hard time returning to civilian life, such as problems sleeping, fears, or reactions when exposed to loud noises or flashes of light?"

"You're asking me if I'm some loony tune?"

"A lot of soldiers have trouble adjusting after combat. It's not uncommon for them to face problems."

Randy's attitude turns nasty, even more so than usual. "I don't have any goddamn problems," he snarls. "Don't you dare make me out to be some kind of fruitcake."

Now Lewis gets angry. He doesn't put up with insubordination, either.

"Look here, Mr. Steele. Nobody's calling you names. In case you've forgotten, let me point out you just shot a cop. You'll need all the help you can get. Our defense may well rest on our ability to convince a jury that your judgment was temporarily impaired. Your displays of defiance do show impairment. I suggest you consider the seriousness of the charge and quit looking to start any more fights, either with me or, God forbid, in the courtroom. So, I will ask you again: Have you had any kind of difficulties adjusting to civilian life?"

Now, in a rare moment of contemplation, Randy reflects on his miserable situation. "Um, yeah, I guess so," he stammers.

Lewis ponders whether to go with the temporary insanity defense, triggered by PTSD. Although he will incorporate it into his argument, he decides that a jury may not find his client sympathetic enough.

10

SARAH GRIFFIN

Sarah Griffin is a congresswoman from Texas. As a Democrat, she just squeaked by in a close reelection in a red district of a red state. To be elected to office under these circumstances, regardless of political affiliation, one must show unwavering fealty to the gun lobby, which excels at making threats. They have the resources to convince a gullible public that liberal politicians are out to take away their firearms. To many, this scenario looks worse than if they took away grandma, who may well be far more accurate with a frying pan than sonny boy is with his 9mm.

On a cloudless day, Sarah is holding a meet-and-greet with her supporters in a shopping center parking lot. Since politicians aren't popular these days, there's still plenty of room for folks to park their cars.

"Good afternoon. I'm Sarah Griffin, as most of you know."

The group greets her with polite applause.

"I'm here to ask you for your support in my upcoming reelection campaign for the United States Congress."

The people cheer this announcement. The crowd not only includes supporters, but also employees of the Congresswoman, who are there to gin up the response.

"As you know, I've always fought for each and every one of you, and I will continue to fight for each and every one of you."

They cheer again at this standard boilerplate political speech. She continues to say what politicians are expected to say while the crowd also responds in the expected way.

"If reelected, I will continue to fight for you, and for the United States Constitution, especially the Bill of Rights."

The crowd applauds, though few of them have ever read the Bill of Rights. Still, it sounds like something important and patriotic.

"I will fight for your First Amendment rights."

The assembled respond with tepid applause.

"I will fight for your Second Amendment rights."

Now the crowd goes wild. In a red state, this is everybody's favorite right. Although many don't understand the concept of free speech, any idiot can pull a trigger.

The cheers drown out Sarah. She finishes with a barely audible "And so forth."

As she continues to bask in the adulation, a clean-cut man with a blank expression works his way through the throng, moving toward the makeshift podium. The congresswoman keeps spewing the standard talking points.

"We're sick and tired of the nanny state. We don't need a government that tramples on our rights! Government regulation is killing jobs. Government regulation values extinct wildlife over the right of Americans to make a living. Government regulation makes it harder for us to defend ourselves and our families from criminals!"

The clean-cut man makes his way to the front of the group, applauding along with everyone else. He unzips the light jacket he's wearing, reaches inside, and pulls out a 9mm semiautomatic with an extended thirty-round ammunition mag. He turns around and opens fire, mowing down several people. The crowd at first looks confused, then panics. Sarah stands frozen, speechless. The gunman aims at her, shooting her in the head.

Meanwhile, another man in the crowd draws his weapon, trying to get a bead on the shooter.

As the gunfire begins, Mike Stuart, who is going through the checkout line of a nearby hardware store, hears the shots being fired outdoors. He draws a handgun and runs out to the parking lot. There he finds complete mayhem while continuing to hear gunshots. The first person he spots is a male in the crowd with a drawn gun who, unbeknownst to Mike, has been trying to stop the original gunman. Mike instinctively shoots that guy instead. As more shots continue to ring out, he now looks shocked as it dawns on him that he has shot the wrong guy.

A seven-year-old girl is the last to be struck down. She gets to be the recipient of bullet number thirty.

As the shooter finally runs out of ammo, he reaches for another thirty-round clip. While reloading, two unarmed men tackle him.

11

THE CAPITOL STEPS

On the steps of the Capitol, a TV journalist is questioning two opposing congressmen, no doubt expecting a complete and utter lack of consensus. Her expectations are soon to be met.

"This is Hanna Ford. I'm here with Democratic Congresswoman Jennifer Schultz from Illinois and Republican Congressman Tom Rowland from Virginia. Congresswoman Schultz, please tell us what it's been like for you and your allies since Sarah Griffin got shot."

Jennifer responds, "Well, as you can imagine, we're all devastated by the event and hope for her speedy recovery when she comes out of the coma."

Tom chimes in, "I'll second that. Her colleagues on both sides of the aisle are sorry and are hoping for the best. Our prayers go out to her and her family."

With perfunctory responses out of the way, Hanna presses further. "As you both know, six other innocent bystanders were killed in the shooting. The gunman got off quite a number of shots due to the high-capacity ammunition magazine. These larger magazines appear to be a common denominator in the most recent mass shootings. Are you, or any members of Congress, reconsidering a prohibition on these?"

Jennifer speaks first. "The ban on assault weapons

and extended magazines expired several years ago. I've long advocated banning these. They're made only to kill as many people as possible. We need to take action on this."

Tom can't contain himself. "Oh please. Whenever we have a mass shooting, you gun control people come crawling out of the woodwork. You're just trying to capitalize on the situation."

Jennifer retorts, "If not now, when? When will you allow this discussion? On your side of the aisle, you always claim it's the wrong time. You want to avoid the subject altogether, kick the can down the road. You guys can't even go to the bathroom without permission from the NRA."

Tom replies, "We don't need more firearm laws. Your side wants to tie the hands of law-abiding citizens trying to defend themselves while making it easier for criminals. It's not fair to Americans who are exercising their constitutional rights. Target shooters, in particular, find it far more convenient to use a larger magazine than to have to keep reloading when they're at the gun range. We shouldn't inconvenience them just because of a few bad apples out there."

Jennifer is incredulous. "What if it saves lives? A young girl was the last one shot. The shooter got stopped only after he ran out of ammunition. If it weren't for these high-capacity magazines, she'd be alive today."

Tom appears unmoved. "That's the price we pay for freedom."

This fires her up more. "Why don't you look that little girl's parents in the eye and tell them that hogwash?"

"I said, now is not the time."

The congresswoman becomes livid. "We'd sure hate to inconvenience you while people are dying! I guess your side of the aisle is too busy to deal with this stuff while you're tied up with more important matters, like outlawing birth control, or whatever!"

At this, Hanna steps in. "OK. I think it's fair to say we won't be litigating this anytime soon. Thanks, and back to you, Wolf."

If there's one thing Congressman Rowland and his colleagues fear more than an assassin's bullet, it's an F rating from the NRA. Congress might run the country, but the NRA runs Congress.

12

THE CHURCH

The Shenandoah Hills Baptist Church sits deep in the South Carolina countryside. Most members live within a small radius. The congregants spend much of their time among themselves, far from the mainstream. They view outsiders with suspicion, healthy or otherwise.

The self-righteous and judgmental Rev. Ronald Wilding leads this church. He sports the de rigueur handlebar mustache and pronounced sideburns that have come to popularity with many of his ilk. When the good reverend isn't preoccupied with bashing the beliefs of others or threatening to burn the Koran, he's busy passing judgment on his own congregation. He has conditioned them through intimidation and upbringing to follow his every proclamation without question.

Rev. Wilding's latest proclamation involves guns. Just allowing the congregants to carry them into the church isn't enough. He goes the extra step and decrees it to be a requirement among the members. He has now conditioned the obedient folks gathered around him to believe he won't admit them to Sunday services unless they're packing a piece. Jesus would be proud.

Ever one to hammer home a point, Rev. Wilding delivers his sermon on this day of the Lord.

"I'm glad you all could make it here today, as this

marks a special occasion in the history of this great church. In fact, the turnout looks sizable, as our recent pro-gun policy has apparently attracted new congregants. From this moment forward, all attendees will be not only encouraged but obligated to carry firearms to our services."

He raises the Bible. "This goes beyond the Second Amendment. It's about our God-given right to bear arms. Let the liberals, secularists, and Communists whine. We don't seek their approval. We are not here to appease them. We are here to guard our faith against all those who would transgress against us. Furthermore—"

He is interrupted by John Smalls, a longtime congregant with Christ-like features, including long hair and a beard. "Excuse me, Reverend."

The reverend is unaccustomed to interruptions while delivering a sermon. He looks stunned, as if he'd been smacked in the face.

A startled church lady sitting nearby scolds John, murmuring, "Don't interrupt!"

The reverend regains his composure. "No. It's all right. What is it, Mr. Smalls? What is it that's so important it required you to impede my evocation to the congregation?"

John doesn't flinch. Never one to suppress an opinion, he's not about to start now. He stands up to speak.

"Well, Reverend, I don't understand this fascination, this obsession, we have with guns. It's become where we're being not only encouraged but even *ordered* to bring them to church. I refuse to bear a weapon in a house of the Lord."

Another congregant, Zeke Watson, jumps in.

"You heard him, John. If you want to attend services, you must carry a firearm."

Rev. Wilding decides now might be the time to show grace before the situation devolves further. "Mr. Smalls has been a welcome member of this congregation for years. We can make an exception. The rule will apply to new congregants."

Another churchgoer, Emma Jones, speaks up. "I'm not sure I feel comfortable with that, Reverend. If we're encouraging total strangers to walk in here with guns, who knows who might show up? I mean, we don't know everybody. Someone may be up to no good."

Zeke responds, "That's the whole point of allowing weapons here in the first place, Emma. If a stranger came in here to cause a problem, we'd all be armed and could deal with it."

John asks him, "Oh, how? What if I'm sitting here in the middle between you and the bad guy? I don't want to get hit with the crossfire. Should I draw my weapon and figure out who to shoot?"

Zeke shoots back, "Look, John, if you don't like it, you can leave. We'll carry guns and worship the Lord Jesus without you."

Rev. Wilding steps in. "Zeke…John…you've both made your thoughts known."

Another devotee, Ben Wallace, rises to speak. "John's got a point. Bullets don't always go where they're supposed to. I used to be in law enforcement and can talk from experience."

Now the whole church is getting riled up. Zeke interjects, "If only Jesus had a gun to protect himself, he might still be alive."

Rev. Wilding greets that statement with a befuddled look. Despite the upset, most of the congregants chuckle at that one.

John continues. "I thought we referred to ourselves as 'people of faith.' Is this how we show our faith? I say this shows a lack of it. Now we can't even step into the Lord's house without carrying a weapon. Where's the faith in that?"

Rev. Wilding has had enough of this sensible argument and counters it by reverting to his original line of nonsense. "To reiterate, I expect all God-fearing members of this church to carry a gun with them at all times. We should fear more than just God. We need to fear others too."

Yes, the good reverend has resorted to that most popular of motivators, one designed to keep congregations throughout history from getting out of line: fear. Its absence cuts both congregational sizes and firearm industry profits. Stay fearful and give us your money.

The real danger, as is so often the case, lies within. It turns out not to be a church invader or an errant parishioner who eventually does in the Rev. Wilding. His demise occurs at the hand of his own wife, who has had enough of her husband's philandering with young female members of the congregation. One day, the honorable Mrs. Wilding cuts down her hypocritical stain of a husband with a .44-caliber revolver. It's been in the family for decades, handed down through generations. For the reverend and his spouse, this firearm won't ever be used to repel trouble. Rather, it will cause a world of it for the parties at both ends of the gun. How typical that is. Now Mrs. Wilding has ended up in prison, while one can only speculate as to where her late husband currently resides.

13

JOE STUPNIK

Joe Stupnik has always been angry. His mother tells him he was born that way, leaving herself out of the equation. His circle of friends has fallen to a grand total of zero. In his mid-thirties, he has until this point lived a most unremarkable life. He has done so without the presence of a father, who split when Joe was four years old. Joe still lives in a small suburban home with his mom. Neither of them socializes much.

Joe spends his weekdays stocking boxes in the local electronics megastore. At work, he keeps to himself, avoiding any interaction with his fellow workers. As many of us seek purpose, he has found his. It's the weekends he lives for. This is when he gets to spend his time at the shooting range. Here he has met his true love: guns.

He spends hours blasting at paper targets. They represent objects in his life. Sometimes they may be his boss, sometimes his coworkers, sometimes a guy who cut him off in traffic, and sometimes even his mother. Joe takes great pleasure in blowing them all to smithereens. He finds satisfaction in putting holes in all the obstacles that make him miserable. However, once they're all destroyed, he's still distraught. What guys like him overlook, however, is that the number-one obstacle making their lives pitiful exists within. Joe's real problem stares him in the face every morning.

This evening, he sits on the couch, zoning out in front

of the TV. A news reporter is describing a grisly scene from outside a movie theater in Aurora, Colorado.

"There are reports of casualties everywhere. A lone gunman, armed with a high-capacity assault rifle, mowed down a theater full of moviegoers at the midnight showing of the new Batman movie."

Joe talks back to the TV. "What do you expect, you douchebag?"

He's enjoying the news way too much, grinning at the depictions of carnage and hysteria. This is much more fun than watching a stupid reality show. He takes this opportunity to lecture the reporter. "That's what you get for trying to ban the public from carrying guns to the movies, you idiot! You guys always want to blame it on the firearms. If they'd allowed more guns in there, people could fire back."

He then grabs an unloaded pistol and points it at the TV. "Man, if only I was there."

He pulls the trigger. The empty gun makes a loud click. Joe sets it down and picks up the remote, going straight to *Right-Wing News*, where Lou Hennesy is interviewing Jim Savage. Besides singing rock and roll, Savage also serves on the board of United Gun Owners, known as UGO. This gives him the opportunity to assault even more than just the eardrums of his fans. His latest endeavor is the authoring of a series of illustrated children's books extolling the joys of pumping a round through a live buck.

Hennesy is providing his usual easy setup. "You know all the liberals out there will use this incident as an excuse to pass more gun control laws. It happens every time we have a mass shooting. It reveals their callousness. This is the wrong time to bring up gun control. A bunch of people just got shot."

Jim jumps right in. "These left-wing commies will take any opportunity to grandstand over a pile of dead bodies. I say this shows more than ever the need for everyone to carry a piece so they could fire back when the situation arises."

Joe obviously isn't the only insane gun owner out there. Even with the PA system switched off, you can always count on Jim to produce a mind-numbing level of feedback. Of course, Hennesy agrees with him.

"It's too bad you weren't there. I'll bet that guy wouldn't have had the chance to shoot more than a dozen people before you brought him down."

"I'd bank on that, Lou."

Jim then turns to another issue that he is also passionate about, besides choking on fresh venison. "There's no doubt these gun grabbers would like to overturn the 'stand your ground' law. They're trying to trample on our Second Amendment rights. They're eroding our freedoms, turning the United States into a nation of Communists. If our forefathers didn't want to let us stand our ground, we'd still be speaking English with an accent—or French, God forbid! Hell, *we* would have been the ones ending up on reservations instead of the Indians."

In an attempt to bring Mr. Savage somewhat closer to planet Earth, Hennesy tries to return the conversation to the topic at hand. "Jim, could you please explain to the audience the difference between armed self-defense and the 'stand your ground' defense?"

"Sure, Lou. Yes, you could carry a weapon to defend yourself before they passed this law. However, you were still expected to back down from a confrontation. The 'stand your ground' law simply means you no longer need to avoid a conflict, that you can deal with it right there. Ultimately, it's all about pride. To back down and walk away from a confrontation can devastate a man's ego. Thanks to the new 'stand your ground' law, a man can once and for all stand up for himself, rather than avoid a violent situation like some coward."

To the total shock of his audience, Hennesy then asks a pertinent question. "What happens in a situation where both parties appear to be standing their ground?"

Savage has a ready response, though not as the result of careful contemplation. "In a case like that, the benefit of the doubt goes to the last man standing, who's in a far more persuasive position to defend his actions."

Joe's mother calls out from the other room, "Why do you listen to this garbage?"

Joe yells, "Shut up and leave me alone!"

"I'll leave you alone when you move out of this house. It's about time. You're thirty-five. Can't you go meet a nice girl and settle down someplace else? Maybe you could find one who would allow herself to put up with the same nonsense you're watching now."

Joe just sits there, fuming. He switches off the TV, goes to his room, and puts on camouflage pants, a tan T-shirt, and a hunting jacket. Storming out of the house, he pulls open the squeaky door of a rusted old Chevy and slams it shut. He screeches out of the driveway, almost hitting an oncoming car.

Despite it being around ten o'clock at night, there are many cars on the road. In his typical foul mood, he weaves in and out of traffic while cussing out the other drivers. One of them cuts him off.

Joe pulls alongside and lowers his window. "Hey, asshole! Watch where the fuck you're going!"

The other driver glares back at him, flipping the finger.

That response sets Joe off even more. He continues to shout, "You want a piece of me, dude? How about you pulling over in that parking lot? Come on, you chicken shit!"

As he shouts, Joe reaches inside his jacket. Sensing he

may be tangling with some crackpot, the other guy speeds off.

Up ahead, Joe spots a nightclub. It's the Slide Inn. He parks, eyeballing the bouncer on the way in. The place is noisy and crowded. He takes a seat in the corner as the bartender walks over. "What'll it be?"

"Give me a glass of water."

"Oh, are you a designated driver or something?"

"No."

At the other end of the bar, Jeff Barnes sits with his girlfriend. They appear to be close and romantic, an island in the sea. Nobody is bothering them, and they are bothering no one.

Jeff motions the bartender to come over. "Hey, man. I'll have another round. She will, too."

The drinks get delivered. As Jeff opens his jacket to grab his wallet, the bartender spots a holstered gun. He feels obligated to speak up. "You know, you're not supposed to be drinking in here while you carry a piece."

Jeff is unapologetic. "I'm behaving myself."

The bartender smiles at him. "Don't worry. I won't tell on good tippers."

He and his girlfriend continue to drink. They're laughing, having a fine time, oblivious to everyone else around them.

Joe has been eyeballing them from his perch at the other end of the bar. He continues to stare. The happier they appear to be, the more sullen he becomes. He's antisocial, alone, and carries a giant chip on his shoulder. The couple represents everything he knows he'll never have.

The bartender comes over to him. "Did you come here to drink water all night?"

Joe opens his jacket, showing his gun. "I can't order

booze in here while I'm carrying this, at least not until they change the laws in this state."

"So you'd rather have a gun than a beer?"

Joe doesn't answer. He glares at the bartender, who's now getting perturbed.

"Look, man. My boss will chew me out for letting somebody take up a seat at the bar all night without paying a dime."

Joe reaches into his pocket. "Here's a quarter. This should cover your water bill. You can pull your tip out of that, too."

The bartender flips the coin to the floor, turns on his heels, and walks away, muttering expletives. With that, Joe goes back to staring at the couple. They are too preoccupied to notice him.

After more than an hour, the couple decides to head home. Jeff helps his girlfriend with her coat. They leave a nice tip for the appreciative bartender.

Joe, who has been watching them like a hawk, moves over just enough to bump Jeff as he passes by. He snaps at Jeff, "Hey! Watch it, pal!"

Jeff isn't looking for any trouble. "Sorry, man." He continues on his way.

This won't do for Joe, who refuses to waste any opportunity for a confrontation. "You *should* be sorry, asshole."

Jeff turns around again, incredulous that this little guy seems so desperate to start a fight. "What?"

"You heard me, you fucking retard."

Stunned, he takes one step toward Joe, who pulls out his gun and pumps two rounds into Jeff's chest. As Jeff slumps to the floor, Joe realizes this is much more exciting than shooting at paper targets, which will never again hold the same allure.

14

JERRY STEPHENS

While Lewis Darby meets with his client Randy Steele, Joe Stupnik is in a similar jailhouse meeting room on the other side of town. Across the table from him sits another criminal defense lawyer, Jerry Stephens. Jerry has more of a mixed record than Darby. This makes him more affordable.

As Jerry thumbs through the police report, Joe sits fidgeting away, his underlying defiance remaining intact. Any feelings of remorse are absent.

"Tell me what happened, Joe."

"Well, I was in this bar, minding my business, when this guy comes over and for no reason pushes me."

Jerry is already skeptical but, like most criminal defense lawyers, expects his clients to describe the situation that landed them in jail in the most innocent of terms. Nobody ever admits any kind of guilt. He has even made a promise to himself: If the day comes when a client admits guilt, he'll reward this person by representing him gratis. Today, isn't the day.

"So, this guy walks up to you and pushes you for no reason?"

"That's right."

"Why do you think he did that?"

"I dunno. Maybe he didn't like my looks. Who knows? A lot of guys out there are looking for trouble."

Although he tries not to bait his clients, Jerry can't always resist. He's sure a prosecutor won't go easy on someone like this. He figures it will be better to push his client here before they rough up the guy in court.

"Nobody does something for nothing. So, I will ask you again—did you contribute to the situation?"

Now Joe gets mad. "I didn't do anything! I was sitting at the bar, drinking a glass of water, keeping to myself."

Jerry sees the need to ease up on his touchy client. "OK, I believe you. Don't take what I ask personally. You must tell me the facts so I can best represent you. The prosecutor won't be as nice as I am, so you need to prepare yourself to handle tough questions."

Joe, now grasping the picture, replies, "Fair enough." He's still agitated. "I don't understand why I need to answer questions at all. I thought the 'stand your ground' law meant I can shoot somebody and go home."

"Sorry, but we do have a legal system. Until the gun lobby totally gets their way, people will be expected to answer questions whenever they shoot somebody. OK?"

"Yeah, sure."

"So this guy, for whatever reason, came up to you and pushed you."

"You heard right. He pushed me."

"When he pushed you, what did you do?"

"Nothing. I did nothing at all. He caught me off guard."

"Did you say anything to him after you made contact?"

"I don't remember. I might have said, 'Excuse me,' or something."

"That was all you said to him? Are you leaving anything out?"

"No."

"What happened next?"

"I dunno. The guy just gives me this real menacing look and comes toward me with his fist raised, like he's gonna hit me."

"Did he strike you?"

"No. I don't need to wait for stuff to happen. I know the law! You're allowed to stand your ground."

"You can if you're in imminent danger. Was that the situation? Were you afraid for your life?"

"Well, yeah. This guy was bigger than me. What am I supposed to do, sit there and let him beat me up?"

"No, you don't have to let him beat you up. My concern is that none of the witnesses seem to back up your side of the story. Nobody saw you get attacked."

"This doesn't mean it didn't happen." Joe is proud of making that existential observation. "It's their word against mine. What if they're friends with this guy? They're just going to lie anyway."

Jerry nods in agreement. "That will be enough for now."

"So I'm gonna walk?"

"It would be unprofessional of me to make such assurances. Let's say our case looks good. The police report claims the guy you shot had an elevated blood alcohol level. He also carried a weapon, which is illegal to do while you're drinking in a bar."

This information startles Joe. Jerry notices this and asks, "Why are you surprised? Did you know he was carrying a gun?"

"Um, no."

"Well, for this case, we'll assume you did. That gives extra weight to our argument."

"Whatever you say, boss."

15

ANGELICA ROBINSON

It's a hot afternoon in the city. Lawrence Peters is standing on the sidewalk, providing curbside business to a steady stream of customers. Most of them are from the suburbs, and they're driving nice, late-model cars through an area that displays less-than-stellar automotive examples in the local driveways. It is, in fact, one of the most dangerous parts of town.

Lawrence is not there to give stock tips, and he doesn't appear to be managing a hedge fund. However, he is making use of nearby hedges and shrubs to hide his product. Smart enough not to handle the drugs himself, he has enlisted the help of twelve-year-old Charlie Post. Charlie approaches the driver-side windows of the cars pulling up to the curb. They hand him the money, and he hands them the goods. Today, it's commerce as usual.

The police ride by once an hour. They're aware of what's happening, but have become too jaded to bother. They've learned from prior experience that any drug arrest they make results in seeing the arrestee back on the street and in business within 24 hours. Besides, if the dealer remained in custody for any length of time, someone would replace him. They figure it's better to keep the devil they know in their sights, so, they cruise by. They'll settle for peace and quiet while they enjoy their donuts and coffee.

Angelica Robinson, a precocious twelve-year-old, has

always made the best of her surroundings. Raised in a tough neighborhood, her parents more than compensate for a lack of resources by giving her an abundance of love and guidance. Excelling in school, she seems to be untouched by the desolate area. She is living proof that the joy and innocence of childhood can overcome most any circumstance. However, there are days where the sinister may intrude. This is one such day.

Angelica lives in a tenement a few blocks from where Lawrence conducts his business. It's Saturday, so she has extra time. Being a model student, she has already done her homework for the weekend, and is out with her friend Trisha, just ambling and talking about boys, school, the usual stuff.

Trisha's cell phone rings. It's her mother, who summons her. She says goodbye and trots off.

Now walking alone, which her parents have warned her not to do, Angelica heads for home. Her father has also warned her not to walk past the intersection where Lawrence has set up his crack-selling enterprise. However, she isn't in the mood to go back around the block in the opposite direction. Instead, she takes a shorter route that involves cutting through the forbidden territory.

Lawrence has been having a busy day. The driver of every other car is looking to make a purchase. At one time, he has had three customers lined up at once for curbside service. His little protégé has been getting a good workout.

Most of the traffic is moving in the same direction, right past Lawrence. However, at some point, a vehicle pulls to the curb on the opposite side. Lawrence calls to Charlie, pointing him to cross over to the waiting customer. He's almost there when Gerald Henley steps out from between two buildings. Gerald is a rival of Lawrence. As business rivalries can be deadly in this line of work, his sudden appearance is unwelcome. First, he barks at Charlie, "Get your punk ass back across the street!"

Not looking for a confrontation, Charlie runs away as instructed. He looks to his boss, not knowing what to do.

This is a situation that won't end well. The two rival drug dealers glare at each other. Gerald has taken the bold initiative to muscle his way into new territory. He has seen too many gangster films and figures this is how it's done. Nobody in his world makes polite requests. He is the first to open his mouth.

"I said don't come around. I'm taking this intersection. You go find yourself another one, bitch."

Lawrence, who has seen his own share of gangster films, isn't about to put up with such talk.

"This ain't your corner. This is mine. *You* get the fuck out of here."

As he speaks, Lawrence is already drawing a 9mm semiautomatic, the official weapon of choice for crack dealers. He points it and fires at Gerald, who ducks behind a car while pulling a similar gun of his own. As shots are being exchanged, the cars speed off, and pedestrians scatter in all directions.

Unfortunately for Gerald, the car he was using for cover is one that speeds off. He's now exposed, out in the open and firing with desperation. Worse still, another sitting duck is about to join him, as Angelica rounds the corner. She is wearing earphones, listening to music on her iPod, oblivious to the action taking place around her.

As she walks behind Gerald, a bullet fired by Lawrence hits her in the neck. She cries out and falls. As Gerald turns to see what happened, he, too, gets shot.

16

THE ROBINSON HOME

Sam Robinson sinks into the couch, holding his wife, Mary. They are devastated over the loss of their daughter Angelica. Detective Larry Strohl sits in a chair across from them. This is the least favorite part of his job. He is jotting down notes.

Sam breaks the silence. "How could they kill my little girl? Angie wouldn't hurt a fly. She never got into trouble. She was perfect. How could this happen?"

Mary struggles to maintain her composure. "My baby's gone! What for? God, please tell me what for?"

The detective grasps for the right choice of words. Despite having made many similar visits during his career, it never gets easier. Delivering horrible news like this could be the most miserable, thankless task in all of creation. "I'm sorry about your loss."

Sam wants to know all the details. "What happened? How'd this happen?"

"Your daughter walked into the middle of a shootout. She was an innocent victim caught in the crossfire."

"Who was shooting at who?"

"It appears the dispute started between two drug dealers, fighting over turf."

Sam pleads with him, "Tell me they're both going to fry. Tell me that much."

"Well, sir, it's not that simple."

"Not that simple? My baby's dead! What's not so simple about that?"

"Sir, if I had my way, they'd both hang by sundown, but we've got these new laws. They complicate things."

"New laws?"

"The lone survivor of the shooting claims he was just defending himself from another shooter. By law, this is his right, to stand his ground."

Mary can't stay silent. "What about my daughter? What about *her* rights? She didn't carry a gun. Must you carry a gun to get rights in this country?"

Sam refuses to accept such a ridiculous excuse. "Yeah. What about the guy that shot her? Don't tell me he gets to walk."

The detective tries to describe the situation in a matter-of-fact way, even though he knows they will not receive it well. "If a judge rules he was legally defending himself, then the court may decide she was just an unfortunate bystander."

Sam is livid. "Unfortunate bystander? Get the hell out of my house!"

Without saying another word, Detective Strohl leaves. He walks to his car, opens the door, and sits for a good while, pondering his position in the universe. When he signed up for this job, the last thing he expected to be doing was making excuses to the victims' families for having his hands tied. Justice has taken some strange twists. He has always been able to give the survivors at least some comfort in believing the murderers of their loved ones would face retribution. Now, he can no longer offer such assurances. The newest laws, written by gun-lobby puppets, have permitted the guilty to walk free nowhere else on this planet but in America. We've not only allowed every gang member, psycho, and fruitcake easy access to portable weapons of mass destruction, we've also given them a means to act with impunity. Stupidity in motion no longer carries a price. If two minorities shoot each other along with an innocent bystander, nobody cares. If a minority shoots a white guy, he gets sent to prison. If a white guy shoots a minority, he becomes a featured guest on *The Lou Hennesy Show.*

17

JUDGE CORCORAN

Judge Joseph T. Corcoran has been a respected jurist for over thirty-five years. He has had many a variety of criminal stand before him. Randy Steele would represent a new breed of murderer, caught on camera holding a smoking gun while still proclaiming his innocence. Randy also represents a new class of murder defendant, one whose legal defense fund is being bolstered by contributions solicited from the public. He has put up his own website for this purpose. Actually, it's his lawyer who set it up, since the contributions will flow straight into the already well-lined coffers of the law firm. The judge finds this to be poignant, considering that the man standing before him committed the murder of a police officer that was captured on a video witnessed by those sending in donations. This provides an opportunity for certain disgruntled members of the population to vote with their wallets.

Besides the defense and prosecution teams, the courtroom on this day is full of uniformed officers. They are looking mighty sullen and angry. In their eyes, Randy would be better off going to trial for running a child prostitution ring.

Judge Corcoran addresses the defendant. "Mr. Steele, you stand accused of murdering patrolman Charles Morrison. How do you plead?"

Without hesitation, Randy declares, "Not guilty."

The plea is expected. It doesn't raise an eyebrow, even

among the police in attendance. Not only is this a common legal tactic, but an indicator of the guilt-free society in which we live. Everybody has an excuse for everything. No one bears any sense of responsibility.

A bailiff leads him back to his seat at the defense table. Randy, who's wearing an orange jump suit, shuffles along with his hands and feet in manacles.

The judge announces, "This is a preliminary hearing to establish conditions for bail."

The mere utterance of these words elicits a loud murmur from the packed courtroom. The police in attendance appear stunned that bail would even be a consideration for an accused cop killer.

The judge hits the gavel. "I want quiet and order. Anyone who chooses to act otherwise will be ejected." He turns his attention back to the participants. "Will the prosecution and defense please approach the bench?"

Addressing the two men now standing before him, the judge says, "We're not here today to try the case, but to determine whether the defendant meets the qualifications for bail. I want you both to confine your arguments to that subject alone."

They resume their places. The judge asks, "Mr. Darby, is there any reason I should even consider bail for the defendant?"

Lewis responds, "Yes, Your Honor, there is. My client has not denied the details of the case. However, we believe he was acting in legal self-defense."

At this, the prosecutor cannot contain himself. "This man shot a police officer in cold blood. He's confessed to it. We have it on dash cam. That anyone who's murdered an on-duty policeman would even qualify for bail of any sort is preposterous."

The judge snaps, "I'll determine that...and I'll thank you not to address the court until I direct you to."

After shooting a smug look at his counterpart, Lewis continues. "Your Honor, my client had good reason to believe he was in imminent danger. He was in fear for his life and for the safety of his wife."

Once again, the prosecutor isn't about to stand by while the defense offers this fictitious version of events. "You can't be serious! This man's a cop killer!"

Judge Corcoran, always one to keep a tight rein on his court, now snaps at him, "Settle down, or I'll hold you in contempt." Turning back to Lewis, he says, "Please continue your argument."

"Under the statutes of our state, any person with a permit to carry a weapon can legally defend himself if he believes his life is in imminent danger."

The prosecutor blurts, "Not from a cop!" This remark gets him another gavel.

Lewis continues. "Your Honor, the law does not specify the nature of the threat. It makes no reference to whether that threat is coming from a person wearing a uniform or not. The 'stand your ground' statute says one may defend oneself, by any means, if one feels threatened."

Now the judge allows the prosecution to respond. The prosecutor is in a foul mood and not about to moderate his response. "Your Honor, this argument being made by Mr. Darby could be the most ridiculous I've heard in my entire career. This line of reasoning could become an excuse for every two-bit hood out there to go around shooting at the police, then claiming self-defense!"

To this, the judge has a sympathetic ear. However, his calling is not to show sympathy, but to administer justice. He thus responds, "As much as I hate to agree with the position of the defense, I am bound to take it into consideration."

The prosecutor looks like someone slapped him in the face. "Your Honor, that argument is outrageous!"

"My job isn't to make the law, but to interpret and enforce it. If you have a problem with that, you should carry it to the state legislature. Personally, I wish somebody would." He then addresses the courtroom with obvious resignation in his voice. "Bail is set for two hundred thousand dollars." He hits the gavel and gets up to leave.

This riles up everyone in the room. The police are furious about the low amount, let alone any bail at all. The judge, who scurries through a side door to the sanctity of his chambers, can't wait to crack a waiting fifth of twelve-year-old scotch.

The bailiffs hustle Randy from the courtroom. He grins at the angry policemen on the way out. One of them yells at him, "You'd better watch your back, asshole."

His colleagues, though sympathetic, quiet him down. The judge pretends not to notice.

18

JOE IN COURT

Joe Stupnik sits with his lawyer in an empty courtroom. He's acting nervous and defiant, which is how he acts most of the time. Only in America are we eager to arm a guy like that.

There is no jury, as many cases such as this are conducted these days as mere bargaining between the defense and prosecutor before a judge. After flipping through a few pages of notes about the case, the judge speaks. "This is a preliminary hearing on the defense's motion to dismiss. Does the prosecution have anything to share with the court?"

The prosecutor replies, "Your Honor, according to witness statements, Mr. Stupnik shot Mr. Jeffrey Barnes without provocation."

Jerry Stephens wastes no time in responding. "Your Honor, the statements conflict. The bar where the alleged incident took place was loud and crowded. If words were exchanged, the noise would have drowned them out. The deceased had been drinking, whereas my client complied with the law and had nothing more than a glass of water."

The prosecutor responds, "That doesn't give him a license to kill. Not everyone can handle their water." He couldn't resist throwing in that last comment.

Jerry doesn't bat an eye. "Florida law states that any individual permitted to carry a firearm can defend himself if he feels threatened. In a sworn statement to the arresting officer, my client expressed fear for his physical safety. Under the laws of this state, he's justified in using deadly force to stand his ground."

This argument dismays the prosecutor. In his twenty years of handling such cases, he has always made a slam-dunk prosecution of any shooting done in public, especially when there were scores of witnesses. He is beside himself. "Your Honor, the defense claims it possesses the power of judge, jury, and executioner. I suppose the court is no longer needed in the dispensation of justice."

Jerry says, "You can characterize it any way you like. However, the law clearly gives my client those powers."

As the prosecutor responds, the judge cuts him off with a wave of the hand. He, too, has seen the police report and reviewed the details of the case. It's obvious to him that this new law opens a massive can of worms. He knows further motions will be a waste of his time.

"In most civilized societies, the argument made by the prosecution would seem perfectly rational. However, the politicians that write these laws place little value on rationality. Therefore, as the 'stand your ground' law is written, I'm inclined—rather, I should say, bound—to agree with the defense. Case dismissed."

The judge hits the gavel. The prosecutor's jaw hits the floor. Joe hits the road.

19

LAWRENCE PETERS

In a downtown courtroom, a hearing is underway for Lawrence Peters, accused of murder in the shooting deaths of Gerald Henley and Angelica Robinson. Sam and Mary Robinson huddle together, holding each other tight. Sam sits in stoic silence while Mary cannot hold back sobs. The hearing is to determine whether the charges against Lawrence should be dismissed, per a motion filed by his lawyer.

The judge has spent the day in chambers with the prosecution and defense. The prosecutor has offered every kind of plea deal he can think of. He hopes to spare the parents of the deceased the agony of being dragged through a long and upsetting trial. However, Lawrence's attorney won't even accept a jaywalking charge against his client. To the incredulity of all those present, his crack-dealing client has a legal concealed-weapons permit. That, combined with the 'stand your ground' law, has handed people such as Lawrence a license to kill. There will be no deal.

As court is gaveled into session, both prosecution and defense approach the bench. Their conversation is hushed. The judge tells them he has made a decision, and they are to maintain order and decorum. The prosecutor, looking crestfallen, expects the worst. As the gun lobby has been involved in writing, or rather overturning, most statutes pertaining to firearm use, his hands have been tied. Citizens of the state are now getting away with murder, both figuratively and literally.

The judge addresses the court. "Mr. Peters, you may be morally responsible for the deaths of two people. However, we are here today only to determine your responsibility in the eyes of the law. I've examined the evidence and heard from both sides. While I find your actions reprehensible, I must make my ruling in accordance with the laws of this state.

He continues. "In the murder of Mr. Gerald Henley, I rule to drop the charge, as you were legally defending yourself under the 'stand your ground' statute. Regarding the case of Miss Angelica Robinson, this court rules that the killing was accidental, taking place during the course of your legal self-defense. Therefore, as difficult as it has been for the bench, all charges against you are hereby dismissed."

Lawrence jumps up, laughing and pumping his fist in the air. Devastated, the Robinsons cry out. Lawrence hugs his attorney, then turns to the Robinsons and shrugs, in no way showing the slightest remorse. "You two have a nice day," he says with a sneer.

Sam has had enough. He jumps over the rail and lunges straight for the defiant Mr. Peters. The bailiffs pull him back.

The judge barks at the defense attorney, "Get your scumbag client out of my sight before I choke him myself!"

No one in the courtroom can blame Sam for the outburst. As for the prosecutor, he would be glad to look the other way if Sam snapped the guy's neck.

20

SAM AND EUGENE

On the evening of the acquittal of his daughter's killer, Sam Robinson is sitting inside with his brother Eugene, sipping a bourbon. "I shouldn't have let Angelica go out alone," Sam says.

Eugene tries to offer solace. "Come on now, you know better. You were a good father. You can't control the world."

"The world's become godless. No one's in control. I should have moved us out of this neighborhood."

"To where? There are problems all over. Kids are getting shot in the suburbs, too."

"It's these damn laws. Folks have carried guns for a long time. When it was illegal to carry, people still did, but they were careful about pulling one out, 'cause they knew they'd be in the wrong. Now they give 'em a license, making it OK to pull the gun."

"It was never OK. Not then, not now. Guns don't bring protection. They bring trouble. They hand you a permit. Now you can carry that gun and pull the thing out whenever you want to. It's like they're giving everyone a badge."

"Oh no. It's worse than a badge. If you got a badge and you shoot somebody, you've still got to answer to someone. With a permit, you ain't got to answer to nobody. The guy that shot my daughter, he's still got his gun, and he's still got his permit. He can live to shoot another day."

Eugene looks stunned. "They didn't take away his permit? What's wrong with these people? This guy's out there dealing drugs. How'd he get a permit?"

"According to the prosecutor, they've busted this guy four times. They got him twice for selling crack, once for breaking and entering, and once for assault.

"And they still let him carry a weapon?"

"Every time, he's plead it down to a misdemeanor. Every damn time. A criminal can still get a concealed-carry permit as long as he beats a felony conviction. We've got criminals walking the streets legally carrying a firearm. In fact, if they get caught in the act, now they can shoot their way out and claim it was self-defense."

"Sam, who the hell's making these stupid laws?"

"They're made by the people that make guns and sell guns. It's all about the money. These bastards don't care if you're protecting yourself or your family. All that matters is the cash. The more guns they sell, the more they rake in. It doesn't matter where that buck comes from, as long as it ends up in their pocket."

Eugene shakes his head. "A few people take in big money, and everybody else pays for it."

A few weeks later, a congressional panel charged with investigating inner-city gun violence invites Sam to speak. The ostensible focus is to stem proliferation of handguns among gang members, many of whom are underage.

Republicans on the committee appear unmoved by Sam's loss. One of them suggests the whole thing is his fault for choosing to live in an undesirable neighborhood. Another points out that Angelica's killer was exercising his Second Amendment right to self-defense. His all-American right to deal crack on the street corner is left out of the conversation. They agree it's unfortunate Angelica was in the wrong place at the wrong time.

As expected, one of the Republican congressmen tells Sam, "Our prayers go out to you and your family." This is the most typical, pandering line uttered to victims' families by those who would otherwise refuse to even lift a finger to protect anyone. Prayers are easier and cost less money.

In the ensuing weeks, Sam will receive an abundance of hate mail and phoned death threats. He incurs this wrath for having the audacity to threaten the God-given Second Amendment rights of the fine American citizens making these threats.

21

THE STUPNIK HOME

It's nighttime at the Stupnik home. Joe sits in his usual spot on the couch with the remote control, surfing through one violent scene after another. In his other hand, as is often the case, he holds an unloaded gun, pointing it at the screen and muttering. He stops at a news channel, which is reporting on the latest outrage du jour.

The announcer, in his most serious tone, is reading, "Upward of seventy people were shot while attending the midnight showing of *The Dark Knight Rises*. Residents of Aurora, Colorado, are still trying to deal with this senseless act. Meanwhile, a spokesman for the gun lobby attacked anyone who would dare exploit this tragedy by calling for tighter gun laws. He insisted armed patrons could have fired back and that they might have reduced the number of victims to maybe only fifty or sixty."

Joe speaks to the tube. "You're damn right it would help. Man, if only I was there."

He points his empty gun at the TV and pulls the trigger, then switches channels. Some woman is arguing with her boyfriend.

Joe continues. "That's right, bitch. You got a problem with me?"

He again aims the gun, pulls the trigger, and punches the remote.

To his next virtual victim: "Oh, you think you're so tough, don't you? What'd you say? How about if I plant your black gangster ass in the ground? How'd you like that?"

The gun clicks. The channel changes.

"Yeah, officer, you heard right. Go mind your own fucking business. What are you looking at? Fuck you."

He pulls the trigger again.

To folks such as Joe, watching television is practice for the real world. To many, it *is* the real world, except for the so-called reality shows.

22

THE STEELE HOME

This evening, Randy and Nancy Steele are viewing something mindless on TV, the same show that Joe Stupnik's watching across town. Randy sits on the couch, drinking beer and looking ornery. His wife is getting stir crazy. "I need to get out. I can't just sit here."

He responds in his own sweet way. "You ain't going nowhere, bitch. As long as I'm stuck here wearing this goddamn ankle bracelet, you're staying here, too."

Not quite satisfied with the response, she asks, "Why should I suffer? I'm not the one who shot a cop."

Now he snaps into full battle mode. "Oh, yeah? You think you're gonna blame this whole thing on me? If you hadn't spent a fucking hour putting on makeup, we wouldn't have been late for the goddamn movie, and I wouldn't have crashed that red light. You got a lot of nerve whining about being stuck here. This is all your fucking fault, bitch. I should have used *you* for target practice instead of that cop. Next time I will, so shut the fuck up."

This passes for a typical evening at home for the Steeles, whiling away the hours while making pleasant conversation. Nancy has a good mind to testify in favor of the slain police officer. If Randy went to prison for life, it would give her a definite break from the hell he's been putting her through. However, Nancy's so afraid of him she figures if she doesn't play along, he'll beat the rap anyway and then beat her. He's already threatened to murder both her and her lawyer if she ever works up the nerve to file for divorce. Besides, even the other soldiers in his unit feared him enough to not bear witness against him over blasting a group of innocent kids.

23

THE ROGERS HOME

The parents of Marvin Rogers sit together, holding and consoling one another. Tina is the first to break the silence.

"I thought we did everything right. We raised a perfect son. He didn't have a single enemy. What more could we do?"

Emmanuel struggles to respond. "Other than keep him locked inside, there's nothing we could have done. It's like you can't even let a kid leave the house these days. He can be on his best behavior, but somebody else out there might be on his worst."

"Nobody values human life anymore."

"I understand. Instead of appealing to man's better nature, we're catering to his darkest impulses."

Tina cannot quit shaking. "Do you realize what hurts the most? This monster who killed our boy is still out there, giving interviews, making statements like he was some kind of hero, protecting the neighborhood. Folks are taking sides. Some are saying vile things about Marvin, putting it all on him. They're blaming his clothes. They're blaming the way he looked. We can't allow them to do that. We must fight this. People need to be informed. I want them to know our son's life was important. They have to stop turning him into some criminal that got what was coming."

Emmanuel fights to keep control of his temper. "The anonymity of the Internet is what emboldens these ugly trolls. They know they can attack others with impunity. I wish the social media companies would force these cretins to post under their real names. That would help keep the garbage in check."

He does his best to reassure her. "Our attorney has promised me he won't permit this to be swept under the rug. He's not going to let them trash our boy. He'll get the news media in on this. We'll make the whole country aware of what happened. We will find justice and vindicate his memory."

Tina finds little comfort in these words. "That won't bring him back."

24

SAM ROBINSON

Sam Robinson sits in silence, brooding. This is what he's spent most of his time doing since the day Angelica got gunned down. No one can fathom the intensity of his feelings. Her smiling face peers at him from a framed picture across the room. At this juncture, his expression now turns from numb to angry. He gets up from the couch, goes upstairs, opens a dresser drawer, and pulls out a handgun. He heads for the front door.

Mary has been keeping an eye on him. "Where are you going?" she asks.

"Just to the store. I need to pick up some things."

She says nothing as he walks off, though she has picked up a dangerous vibe.

Sam marches down the street, mean and determined. He blocks out all sights and sounds of the neighborhood as his mind is now of a singular focus, heading for the place where his daughter last stood. He has unfinished business.
As Sam rounds a corner, there stands Lawrence Peters. He's standing in the same spot, engaged in the same profession, acting like nothing ever happened. Other than a lack of living competition, everything else is the same.

He waits at the curb, waving the next car over. Sam walks up behind him with a drawn handgun. He raises it as Lawrence turns around. Lawrence takes on a look of sheer terror, as the barrel of a gun is only a few inches away from his face. Sam's got him point blank.

Sam doesn't pull the trigger, but speaks, not wanting to deprive himself of the opportunity to watch Angelica's killer squirm.

"How do you like this? How's it feel, you scumbag? Are you standing your ground now? Is this your ground? This was my daughter's ground."

Lawrence puts his hands up, petrified. He knows the end is near as he stares straight into the barrel of Sam's gun. He wants to beg for his life, but believes it would be a request he doesn't even deserve to make, and therefore remains speechless.

Sam's finger is on the trigger. There is a long period of silence. Lawrence stands with his hands up and his eyes closed, trembling in fear, cringing at what is about to happen.

Nothing happens.

Sam puts the gun down and walks away, disappearing around the corner. Lawrence falls to his knees.

Mary waits for Sam, staring at the door the whole time he has been gone. She expects another knock from a policeman with yet more horrible news. When Sam comes bursting in, she grabs her chest and lets out a loud sigh of relief.

"Well, where'd you go? I don't see anything from the store."

He just looks at her and breaks down in tears.

"What happened?"

"Nothing. Nothing happened." He shows her the handgun.

"Oh no! What did you do?"

"I did nothing. I saw him, saw Angelica's killer, and I put this gun right in his face. I wanted to kill him, I really did, but I stopped."

Mary gently takes the pistol from his hand.

He continues. "When that guy took our baby's life, he damned himself for eternity. I guess if I did this to him, I'd suffer the same fate. I couldn't do it. Much as I tried, I couldn't sink to his level."

She puts her arms around him. "Oh Sam. You did the right thing. You didn't kill him because you're a better man than that. You're a good man, Sam. That's why I married you."

Lawrence Peters is no longer standing at the street corner. The moment Sam put that gun in his face, he had made a silent vow: if God would spare his life, he wouldn't sling another rock of crack.

He keeps that promise for almost an entire hour before returning to his regular post. Maybe God could rest on the seventh day, but money never sleeps.

25

TV GUN DEBATE

A televised skirmish between opposite sides of the gun issue will guarantee to generate a lot of heat while gen-
erating no light whatsoever. One such debate is gearing up
today.

Jane Rivers, the host of a daytime cable talk show, sits
with two spokesmen in opposing camps. Both look downright angry, itching for a fight. After getting the countdown
from her producer, she kicks off the next segment.

"I'd like to welcome Chris Wilson of the Brady Campaign to Prevent Gun Violence and Phillip Austin of American Patriots, a pro-gun rights group. They are here today to
discuss the new 'stand your ground' laws that are sweeping
this country. Chris, why is your organization opposed to this
law?"

As she introduces him, Jane can't help but ponder how
only in America would you find an asinine subject like this to
even debate. Mr. Wilson has come prepared.

"The current laws allow for a person to defend himself or herself. A permit process allowing someone to carry
a firearm is already in place throughout almost every state.
'Stand your ground' takes it to the next level, encouraging the
individual gun owner to serve as judge, jury, and executioner.
We don't feel the average citizen qualifies to function in these
multiple capacities—"

Phillip cuts him off. "Now, hold on there! The Second Amendment clearly states, 'The right to bear arms shall not be infringed.' End of story."

Jane interjects, "By using the term 'end of story,' you're underscoring how many on your side seem to value the Second Amendment over the First. You act like we aren't even allowed to talk about it."

"Well, if they hadn't written the Second Amendment, we wouldn't have a First Amendment, right?"

Chris needles him, "Hey, Phil, try to do more than just regurgitate these dime-a-dozen talking points. This oft-repeated statement implies no one would listen to you if you didn't carry a gun, like it's the only thing that can buy respect."

Jane waves him off, attempting to reassert control. She continues to query Phillip. "So your position is all firearm laws are unconstitutional?"

"You're damn right, they are."

Again, Chris steps in. "What about the 'well regulated militia' clause of the Second Amendment? Why do you think our forefathers inserted it? Does it mean the same thing as 'unregulated' militia? You guys can't even quote the amendment in its entirety, only focusing on the part you like. Here's a news flash for you: the right to bear arms doesn't come without regulation, according to the exact wording of the Second Amendment."

Phillip will cling to political talking points as a sailor clings to the mast in a storm. Mindless repetition is all it takes to sway a mindless public. "I don't know, and I don't care. The right to bear arms shall not be infringed. Besides, our forefathers gave us that right in order to overthrow a tyrannical government."

Chris is ready for this talking point, too. "Is that so?

We get this line all the time from the gun lobby. They say the framers believed the Second Amendment gives license to engage in an armed overthrow of the government. This is also false and always has been, no matter how many times it gets repeated. You people should try reading the Constitution instead of pretending to quote from it."

"I've read it," Phillip snaps.

"You need to read it again. Look for the part that gives citizens the right to bear arms against their own government. It doesn't exist. That would be a recipe for anarchy. Our forefathers weren't stupid enough to allow this. Maybe you should check out Article I, Section 8. It spells out the duty of the 'well regulated' militia referred to in the Second Amendment, which is to put down insurrection *against* the government, not start it.

"For the sake of argument, if one had a grievance with the powers that be, whom can he or she legally shoot under the Constitution? Could he shoot the police? Could he shoot the National Guard? Could he shoot the White House Secret Service detail and then walk inside and shoot the president just because he and his buddies think they have a legitimate beef? Exactly who in this so-called tyrannical government do you suggest they can legally shoot?"

This challenge to his positions renders Phillip speechless. He's used to short, simple arguments that aren't held up to any kind of scrutiny. This is what he gets for allowing someone to ask him questions on any other network but *Right-Wing News.*

Chris presses on. "You guys love to make these ridiculous, over-the-top, grandiose statements, but you never bother to work through the literal implications of them."

Once again, Phillip resorts to repetition. "The right to bear arms shall not be infringed."

Now Jane throws a wrench into his talking points. "Mr. Austin, do you believe children should be able to carry guns to school?"

"What do you mean by 'children'?"

"Oh, say, eleven or twelve years old."

"You aren't serious, are you?

She is, at least as far as addressing the issue. "Well, since you're quoting the Constitution, I should point out the Bill of Rights makes no reference to age. A right is a right. Is that not the case? So if the right to bear arms shall not be infringed, this right must also extend to twelve-year-olds. What say you?"

Phillip can tell he's being boxed into a corner. He stews over how to respond to this obvious trap. One thing he bristles at is a smart woman with a sharp tongue. He again longs for the comfort of *Right-Wing*, where he'll likely encounter neither.

Chris relishes the opportunity to pile on. He goads Phillip into coming up with an answer. "Phil, are you in favor of arming twelve-year-olds, or are you in favor of…" He takes on a sinister tone, "…*gun control*?"

Sidestepping a direct response, which would force Phillip to utter the unspeakable term, he gives a more simple and obvious rejoinder. "I'm not in favor of arming kids."

"So now you think the right to bear arms *shall* be infringed! Our forefathers had good sense to add the 'well regulated militia' clause."

Jane adds, "It was probably put there to guard against armed anarchy. Just because you have a gun doesn't give you the power to be the law unto yourself."

Chris continues with this tack. "You know, Phil, in the early days of this country, young kids carried muskets to school and hunted for the family dinner on the way home.

We should let teenagers carry them. I hear Apple's coming out with a new model that has built-in Wi-Fi."

Phillip gets fed up. "That's right. Treat the whole thing like a joke."

Jane says, "You know, plenty of so-called grownups aren't any more mature than twelve-year-olds. Since you've now acknowledged the need for some form of gun control, Mr. Austin, how about if we weed *them* out, too? Some may not possess the capacity to handle such a responsibility. Do you think people should have to pass a basic mental competency test before they can carry a firearm in public?"

He stands his ground. "The right to bear arms shall not be infringed, especially by some shrink."

Chris takes another dig. "Have you been seeing one, Phil? If not, you might want to consider it."

"Screw you!"

At that, Phillip rips off his earpiece, storming off the set.

Jane faces the camera. "It looks like we're making real progress here, folks."

Chris continues to hector him, though Phillip is out the front door of the building by now. "Come back. This was just starting to get interesting. Where are you going?" He turns to the host. "I hope he's not getting his gun."

26

PARENTS OF MURDERED
CHILDREN

On a Wednesday evening, a crowd packs the high school auditorium. However, there isn't a student in sight. Tonight, the room is full of distraught and angry survivors, along with grieving relatives and friends. The sign outside says *Parents of Murdered Children*. This is a group that has grown over the past few years, starting with a handful of bereaved adults. You'd only find a meeting like this in the United States.

The outer world may act paralyzed at the intractable positions on the gun debate. However, inside the hall, no one is in any mood to hear about the glorious Second Amendment. The people are here following a rash of endless school shootings. They are tired of hearing the excuse, "Nothing can be done."

The first to speak tonight is a representative from the local chapter of United Gun Owners. This is one of several organizations that act threatened and defensive whenever there are incidents of mass violence. They're driven by the fear that every incident may provide the impetus for some new restriction on firearms. They're afraid they might lose the right to pull a gun on anyone who makes them feel nervous. Thanks to associations like theirs, we're now a nation full of skittish people with the ready means to act on their fears. Don't bother telling these folks that the most potent source of their fear lies within.

UGO spokesman Lance Pruitt might as well have stepped on a nest of angry hornets. The people are in no mood for excuses. Many in this group of bereaved parents have experienced firsthand the agony of losing a child to mindless, random gun violence. He attempts to make his case.

"We all know from watching movies and TV, the only thing that can stop a bad guy with a gun is a good guy with a gun. These school shootings will only continue until we allow every teacher to carry a firearm. Furthermore..."

He gets no further into his prepared speech as the crowd in the auditorium erupts in an angry fury. They are in no mood to sit and digest this repetitive nonsense. A man from the front row jumps right into Pruitt's face, only inches away and screaming mad.

"You moron, how the hell do you know a good guy from a bad guy when everybody's got a gun? You think I want my kid sitting in a classroom in the middle of a gunfight between the teacher and some armed imbecile like yourself?"

Pruitt scrambles out of the gathering faster than one of the armored piercing bullets he carries in his arsenal.

After a fair amount of time trying to calm things down, the moderator, a scholarly middle-age woman, restores order. The man who jumped onstage agrees to leave on his own accord. The audience sympathizes, as he has recently lost his only child to a stray bullet as she walked down the street.

The moderator resumes the discussion. "All of us are aware of what gun violence is doing to this country. Yet we act as if we're helpless to do anything about it. It's not just the violent acts themselves, but the overall paranoia in our culture that is driving this. We've turned into an armed society, not to protect ourselves from criminals, but rather to protect ourselves from one another."

The audience murmurs in agreement.

She continues. "The gun lobby wants us all to live in fear so they can sell more guns, which makes them all wealthier. They're trying to make us believe that since they've sold a gun to everyone else, you need to buy one, too. That way, you'll be able to protect yourself from everyone *else* they've sold a gun to—"

A woman in the audience interrupts her. "So, what do we do about it? Who do we vote for? Everybody fears the NRA and UGO. Nobody's standing up to these people. The Republicans have whored themselves out to the gun lobby, and the Democrats have become too spineless to stand up to them, too."

The moderator nods. "Their deep pockets threaten anyone who challenges them. Our representatives fear getting thrown out of office. They're afraid they'll end up buried in an avalanche of negative campaign advertising, especially now that our wonderful Supreme Court has lifted the limits on corporate contributions."

A man speaks up. "Maybe when a few of the super wealthy lose their children to gun violence, then we'll be able to fight money with money. This is what it's all about."

Some of the attendees applaud this statement. The moderator raises her hand to cut off the applause. "Everyone here has felt the pain of that, and I'm sure we wouldn't wish it on anyone. We need to focus on common-sense approaches."

A woman stands up to speak. "I'll tell you a good place to start. A classmate murdered my son in school. So they send this kid to juvenile detention for a couple of years, and that's it. They hold no one else responsible. Who'd he get the gun from? Was it his father? Was it another classmate? Was it a stranger on the street? How come nobody pays for these crimes?"

Another man says, "The gun lobby just wants to give every teacher a gun, like it's that simple. This is their asinine formula! With three hundred million guns already in this country, we're supposed to believe the only solution to the problem is more guns. It's complete insanity!"

Another woman says, "I wish to return to a point made earlier. Why don't we ever arrest those who give these weapons to kids? We seem to want to focus all the blame on the shooter, yet we leave the enabler alone. Shouldn't whoever supplies the kid with a gun be thrown in the next jail cell? Wouldn't that help put this epidemic in check?"

There is a momentary pause as the audience members nod in agreement to what would be such an obvious point in a saner society than ours. The moderator continues.

"You all make good points, which brings me to another idea to consider. If our legislators are too gutless to take action, then we must do it ourselves. We know they no longer represent the majority, so let's have the people speak directly. We need to use the power of citizens' petitions to force these issues onto the ballot, bypassing the cowards that pretend to represent us."

Frank Meadows, a quiet gentleman who has been sitting in the back row, takes this all in. He, too, has lost his beloved granddaughter to the mass shooting at Sandy Hook Elementary School in Newtown, Connecticut. She was the absolute joy of his life. Since losing his wife to cancer, she had been the one thing that kept him going. Her untimely demise at the hands of a crazed gunman has brought more pain than he can bear.

Talk about politicians and petitions might be well intentioned. However, Frank no longer has any patience toward what appears to be an intractable enemy, and he knows what he must do. Whatever he is planning may damn him to hell. This is of no concern, because he's already there. For him, it's time to fight fire with fire.

27

FRANK MEADOWS

Frank Meadows switches off the radio, having heard far more than he can handle. Since attending the *Parents of Murdered Children* meeting the evening before, he has spent the rest of the night behind the wheel. Having received a felony conviction on his record for insider stock trading several years ago, he knows it would prevent him from purchasing a weapon. He figures the solution would be as simple as driving across the state line to Virginia, home to some of the laxest gun laws in the country.

Armed with a Google map printout, he has located the nearest firearms dealer. His timing is fortuitous, as he and the clerk are the only two inhabitants in the shop at this early hour. He pulls an envelope out of his pocket, laying it on the counter.

Frank says, "I have a prior incident on my record that may prevent me from passing a background check. I was wondering if you might skip that part of the sales process for the five hundred dollars cash in here."

The clerk looks at the envelope, then eyeballs Frank. "I'm sorry. It's none of my business what you did in the past, but I can't sell you a weapon. I would be putting my job at risk." After a moment's pause, the clerk asks, "You're not a cop, are you?"

Frank, bleary-eyed from lack of sleep, asks, "Do I look

like a cop?"

The clerk chooses not to answer the last question. He ponders the situation for another moment, asking, "You aren't from around here, are you?"

"No."

"I'll tell you what. Pull the money out of the envelope and drop it on the floor. Then walk out and sit in your car while I make a phone call. Someone should be here soon who can help you out. If you're a cop, you still can't arrest either one of us. It's not against the law for me to make a phone call. It's also not against the law to pick up cash off the ground and put it in my pocket. As far as private sales go, that's legal, and none of my business."

The clerk is on the lookout for some enterprising fed looking to bust a borderline gun dealer. He needn't worry, because nobody around here cares anyway.

Frank understands the instructions, gives him a nod, drops the money on the floor, and walks out of the store. Less than ten minutes after returning to his car, a late-model Cadillac pulls up next to him. The man who gets out is wearing an expensive suit and tie. He could pass for a well-heeled businessman, lawyer, or even a member of the clergy. He strides over to the driver's side door as Frank lowers the window.

The man asks, "Would you like to make a purchase?"

"Yes. I could use some assistance."

"I understand. What sort of merchandise are you looking to buy?"

Frank already knows the answer to that. He plans on buying the same weapon the gunman used to murder his granddaughter.

"I'd like to buy a Bushmaster AR-15."

"How about mags and ammo?"

"I could use five thirty-round magazines, and two-hundred rounds of ammo."

The man does quick math. "Have you got three thousand dollars in cash?"

Frank knows he's getting gouged, but has come prepared. "Sure do." He counts out the money in one hundred dollar bills and hands it to the businessman.

"Wait here. I won't be long."

Ten minutes later, the man walks out of the store with a large box and a bag full of ammo. He instructs Frank to open the trunk. "He only had three mags left." The other two have ended up in the businessman's coat pocket, along with a couple thousand dollars' profit from the purchase.

Frank thanks him and starts his car.

The businessman walks away. After taking a few steps, he turns and comes back to Frank's window.

"Hey, buddy. I don't know what kind of plan you've got, and I don't really care. Whatever it is, do it as far away as possible. There's one more thing. You and I never met. Got it?"

Frank replies, "Got it." He puts the car in gear and drives off.

The businessman knows that look in Frank's eye. He's seen it before. It's the stare of determination to create major damage.

28

FRANK MEETS BILL

As sure as the sun rises, after every mass shooting the public sees another appearance by Bill Fontaine, head of UGO. This organization stands to the right of the NRA, going even further in their advocacy of total elimination of all gun laws. They strike fear in the hearts of Congressmen on both sides of the aisle. Bill's only real function is to make a financial kickback off gun sales, done under the pretense of protecting the Second Amendment. He will attack anything and anyone who dares question the easy availability of high-powered military-grade weaponry to the average schmo. His pockets are also filled with dues paid by average schmoes.

On the drive back, Frank switches from one talk radio station to another. He hears multiple excuse makers from the gun lobby try to pass off the latest mass school shooting as being the fault of Hollywood, video games, and mental illness. A caller, who is summarily dismissed, has the audacity to suggest those who need to keep an arsenal at home also suffer from some form of mental illness. The host, who attacks this person without mercy, exhibits his own cognitive shortcomings, having the inability to engage anyone who dares hold a contrary opinion.

Our forefathers who wrote the Second Amendment should see the unintended consequences of their work and hear some of the inane arguments made ostensibly on their behalf. Then again, they had the good sense to include the phrase "well regulated militia." From minions of the gun lobby, one could assume the line reads "unregulated militia." If we don't need any regulation, then we don't need a Constitution, either. If this sounds like questionable reasoning, then you've grasped the current state of confusion gripping our country.

These thoughts and others pass through Frank's mind as his drive continues well past dusk. He is a man on a mission. At this point, it's all that's spurring him forward, giving him the will to exist. He now lives for only one thing: a face-to-face meeting with his most hated nemesis.

Upon returning, his quest takes on a singular focus. Armed with information gathered from the Internet, Frank discovers the home address of Bill Fontaine, which is just outside the city of Norfolk, Virginia. The residence lies in an upper-scale suburban area amid a honeycombed series of cul-de-sacs. Gun money has provided him great wealth and privacy.

Although the chance of pulling off a successful frontal approach seems questionable, Frank sees a possible opening. As the property stretches all the way to the banks of an inland waterway that flows into Chesapeake Bay, he spots easy and direct access.

As this would appear to be a desperate mission ending either in death or prison, Frank has one infallible asset on his side. He doesn't care. He has no intention of returning from this operation, as it would be his last great statement and a bloody tribute to his fallen granddaughter. The lack of intent to escape with his life makes him invulnerable, bolstering his chance of success. It is the same mind-set of suicide bombers in the Middle East, whose devotion to dying on the field of battle also gives them a heightened sense of invulnerability.

For once, he'll get to use his military training for something constructive.

He parks his car around a mile upriver from the Fontaine estate. It is a short walk to the water, close enough for him to carry a kayak. The Bushmaster is slung over his shoulder. He departs from the bank, guiding the craft downstream at a leisurely pace. It's Sunday, and from prior reconnaissance, he expects to find Bill at home. He docks the boat and climbs up a small slope. Walking into a thick blanket of trees, he applies full camouflage makeup to match the outfit he's already wearing.

Frank approaches the grounds of the property, moving from tree to tree, following a portable GPS tracker. It's a well-apportioned estate. This comes as no surprise, as the generous kickback that UGO receives for every gun sale can buy a nice, ornate hideaway. With a cutter, he creates an opening in the barbed wire fence surrounding the premises. He peers through a pair of binoculars from behind a row of bushes, scouting the rear of the house, looking for the easiest way in. He soon realizes that making a forced entry won't be necessary. There, lying in the middle of the yard on a chaise lounge, soaking up the midday sun, is Bill Fontaine. A handgun sits on a nearby table.

This mission might be easier than he was expecting. Perhaps he will even escape intact. After looking around for witnesses or armed security, he realizes he has made it to this spot undetected. He raises his rifle, drawing a bead, ready to not only shoot Bill but reduce him to Swiss cheese. As Frank focuses his gun site on the prone man, putting him right in the crosshairs, another figure suddenly appears. It's a young girl, who runs across the lawn and jumps into Bill's lap.

Frank freezes. The kid looks to be around the same age as his own deceased granddaughter. This causes a great dilemma. As much as he despises the girl's grandfather, he is hesitant to expose an innocent child to such violence. Besides, she's now directly in his line of fire.

Regardless, he knows there's no turning back. The murderous urge has welled up inside him to such a degree it will not allow him to walk away without fulfilling his mission. Watching the joy on Bill's face as he holds and talks to the little girl, Frank becomes overwhelmed by his own loss. This is more than he can bear. The operation is on.

He steps from behind the bush where he has been hiding, moving rapidly toward Bill. As the distance between the two closes, Bill spots Frank and is overcome with panic. He tries to reach for his handgun, but fumbles it to the ground. He then grabs the girl as a human shield, clutching her tightly to his chest. She screams as he begs, "Please! Don't do it! Don't hurt my granddaughter!"

To see her used as a shield further enrages Frank. "Let go of her! Let go of her, you coward!" he yells.

Bill refuses. It would leave him totally exposed.

Frank doesn't want to harm the child. He walks up close enough to grab her arm, pulling her away. Bill, who's now lying there with his eyes closed, cringes in anticipation. The girl runs off to hide behind a tree.

Frank has his prey point blank, with a thirty-round load and murderous intent. He speaks first. "Nice place you have here, Bill. That blood money you make sure goes a long way."

Bill is whimpering, "Please don't kill me. Please just walk away. I promise not to report this to the police."

Frank steels his resolve. "Not a chance. Say goodbye."

He raises the rifle, but hesitates. He wants to savor the moment, watching this arrogant bastard reduced to a sobbing, quivering, begging mess. Rather than spoil it all by pulling the trigger, Frank subjects Bill to further torment.

"How do you like it, you scared little piece of trash? I guess you're not such a tough guy after all, are you? How do *you* like feeling so helpless?"

Bill cannot respond, as he's frozen in fear.

"Now you have a taste. You're at my mercy, begging for your life. This is just what it was like for my granddaughter, you bastard. She was begging for her life, too. Her only crime was attending first grade, along with her classmates. Some demented asshole with a gun like this, and an ammo mag like this, gunned her down at school. You! You fought for that monster to get a hold of this weapon! You fought for him! You fought to make it as easy as possible for him to end my granddaughter's life, you goddamn piece of garbage! What about *her* rights?"

Frank is through proselytizing. Bill continues to whimper. Maybe telling him off is all Frank needed to do, as he now somehow feels cleansed. Rather than pull the trigger on his helpless target, he throws the gun down in disgust and turns to walk away. At that, Bill reaches for his own fallen pistol, picks it up and, without a word, fatally shoots the unarmed Frank right in the back.

Every news outlet in the Western world and beyond would broadcast such a horrible incident involving a high-profile individual like Bill Fontaine. However, this unspeakable tragedy is kept absent from the media. A couple of phone calls to some powerful connections make the whole thing disappear. Bill could have lost something far more important to him than his own life: his *reputation*. If the public found out the head of UGO fumbled his weapon at such a crucial moment, it could be ruinous to his tenure. Otherwise, shooting an unarmed man in the back is no big deal.

29

ANDY MORRIS

A young couple enters the office of a pediatrician. Tom and Margaret Morris have brought their six-year-old son Andy to see the doctor. Tom is wearing his favorite camouflage jacket. He'd also rather be anywhere else but here, such as out in the woods shooting holes in animals.

The doctor stitches a nasty gash in the boy's hand as an assistant dabs Andy's tears. They comfort him with their reassuring tone.

"There you go, buddy. You'll be all right. Remember to be extra careful around sharp objects, OK? The nurse will finish putting on the bandage. I need to speak with your parents." He turns to address them. "Could you come to my office?"

Tom becomes suspicious. "Is there a problem?"

"No, I want to discuss something."

The father nods, and the couple follow him. At first, they remain standing.

"Sit down, please."

Margaret takes a seat. Tom refuses the request, preferring to deal with the expected confrontation while remaining on his feet. He's uptight and leery.

"I'll stand, thanks. What's so important that you had to call us in here?"

The doctor gives them a stern look. "Despite what you

told my nurse, that cut on Andy's hand wasn't from any butter knife. It had to be a hunting or military knife, something with a serrated edge."

Tom asks, "So, what's the difference? Why does that matter to you?"

"It matters because Andy is my patient. A blade like that is very dangerous. You don't want to let a six-year-old have access to something like that."

Tom snaps, "I didn't put it in his hand! He picked it up on his own."

His wife breaks her usual obedient silence. "You've shown it to him before. He knows where you keep it."

"You stay out of this, Margaret." Then addressing the doctor, the tone of Tom's voice modulates from confrontational to downright menacing. "Look, he's my boy. If I want him to learn about hunting, it's my business, not yours. You got that? Am I coming through loud and clear? If I want to teach him how to handle a knife, that's my right."

The doctor, to his credit, maintains his professionalism. "Of course you have the right. I'm not questioning that. You know how boys are curious about things, and they can climb, so you need to store dangerous objects in a secure place where he can't get to them."

Margaret attempts to make peace. "We'll try to be more careful."

The doctor asks, "Do you keep any firearms in the house?"

Tom again flashes his temper. "Whoa! That's none of your business. I know the laws of this state. You're not even allowed to ask us that!"

The doctor returns fire. "Well, if you promise not to report me to the state, I'll promise not to report you to child services. How about that?"

Tom retorts, "Don't push your luck!"

"The only thing I care about is the health of my patients. I expect those responsible for their welfare to do likewise."

"He's my son, and I'll raise him however I damn well please." He turns to Margaret. "Let's go."

Exasperated, she refuses to rise.

"Now, goddamn it!" He grabs Margaret's hand and yanks her out of the chair and out the door.

The doctor just sits at his desk, shaking his head. He would like to do more, since he finds these situations can always turn from bad to worse. However, his hands are tied. Tom is correct. As the current law reads, doctors in the state of Florida can't broach the subject of firearms in the homes of their patients. In its zeal to protect the Second Amendment, the gun lobby has now declared war on the First. A physician is free to discuss anything else. Sure, he might save a young life, but God forbid it could come at the expense of another firearm sale. Profits take precedence.

30

RANDY AND HIS BRACELET

Lewis Darby is meeting again with Randy Steele, who has turned himself into a minor celebrity since gunning down Patrolman Charles Morrison. Pleading not guilty under the 'stand your ground' defense has garnered him much national attention, especially now that a video of the incident got leaked to the media. Few attorneys would even touch this case. However, in this age of excuses, nothing is any longer impossible.

Lewis asks, "How are you holding up?"

A grumpy Randy responds, "I'll be doing a lot better once you get this damn bracelet off my ankle. I needed consent from the court just to come here."

"I had to fight for that. Fortunately, the judge and I are golfing partners."

"That's great. While you're at it, how about getting me permission to go out for a drink or dinner or something?"

"We'll see. I don't expect him to be any more generous right now in terms of your liberties. We have more important concerns to take care of."

"I thought you said we had a good case."

"We do, but you shot a cop on duty, let's not forget. It's not on the same level as shooting an armed intruder. We've got major work cut out for us. Don't be making any plans to go out drinking and dancing in the meantime."

"With what you're getting paid, you'll forgive me for having high expectations. What are we looking at?"

"Well, the best possible outcome would be a downright dismissal. I've found a few things in Patrolman Morrison's past we could use."

"Such as?"

"He's faced previous accusations of using excessive force and domestic violence. We may cite these incidents as reasons you would have needed to defend yourself. However, some things in your past might work against us."

This causes Randy's face to tighten. "Like what?"

"Like assaulting a police officer, for instance."

Randy snaps, "It wasn't my fault. He was being disrespectful. So I had a few beers. Can't a guy go buy a drink without getting harassed?"

"Well, the prosecution will use that, along with those two domestic violence charges against you."

Randy doesn't appear the least bit apologetic about that. "Who hasn't slapped their wife around a few times? She doesn't always pay attention. You know how women can be." Now he snarls at Nancy, who made the mistake of coming along, "Thanks a lot, bitch. I told you not to go whining to the cops. After all the nice things I bought you, this is how you thank me? If I get sent up because of you…"

Lewis cuts him off. "Look, you need to learn to control yourself. If you conduct yourself in front of a judge the way you're conducting yourself in here, then heaven help us. Your anger at the whole world won't make our case. Do you understand?"

Randy sits there, looking sullen. "Yeah, I understand."

"You may also want to seek professional counseling."

"I'm not going to a goddamn shrink! There's nothing wrong with me. You just worry about doing your job."

In these situations, Lewis wonders if he's doing any-one a favor by fighting to get such hotheads off from charges for which they are clearly guilty. This guy belongs in prison. However, Lewis's professional training guides him to push such thoughts out of his mind, lest they cloud his judgment. Still, he can thank cloudy judgment for sending so many clients his way. It pays well.

31

STEVE COLSON

It's a sunny day in an outdoor suburban park. Afghan war vet Steve Colson is shooting baskets with his twelve-year-old daughter, Katy. The weather couldn't be more perfect. This is a vision come true for Steve, who has slogged through a year of hell halfway around the world. The only thing keeping him sane through the whole ordeal was the hope he would once again reunite with his family at the end of the tour.

He takes careful aim at the basket and makes a long shot. This delights Katy. "Wow! That was great. You're the best."

"No, honey, you are."

He gives her a hug. After spending the last year dodging bullets in Afghanistan, he can't stop hugging his daughter. She is thrilled beyond words at having her father back home and dreads the day when they will send him out for another tour. They cherish any time they can spend together. Nothing is too small to take for granted.

Katy continues to throw the basketball in the general vicinity of the hoop on the chance she might make the occasional shot. Steve decides that a little coaching may be in order. "Let me show you how this is done."

"No, I'll show you!" She grabs the ball and throws it toward the basket, missing again.

Steve calls time out. "No, honey. You can't just throw it and hope it goes through. You've got to concentrate, aim, and release it the right way. Follow what I do."

He lines up, sinking another one. He hands the ball to Katy, guiding and instructing her on how to shoot. She puts up a shot, just missing. "Ah…"

"No, that was good. You're getting it. I want you to learn correct form. You must focus only on the basket, blocking out all other distractions. Remember to follow through on your release. You need to visualize the basketball going through the hoop before you even shoot."

Although somewhat confused by this abstract philosophy, Katy tries it out. She puts up another shot. This one goes in. "Yeah!"

"Way to go! Now you're getting the hang of it. The more you practice, the better you'll get. Just remember to do your homework first."

"Will you be here to teach me? I don't want you to go back to Afghanistan. Mom and I were so lonely when you weren't here."

"Honey, I felt the same way. Every day is special. Never forget that."

"I won't, but things are much more special when you're here."

Two boys, both the same age as Katy, have been riding their bikes through the park. They take them onto the court, circling around the basket at the other end. She waves to one of them. "Hey, Bobby."

They come over to say hello. "Hey, Katy, what's up?"

"My dad's teaching me how to play basketball."

Steve extends his hand. "Hi. I'm Katy's dad."

"I'm Bobby. This is my cousin John."

"It's nice to meet you both. Any friend of Katy's is a

friend of mine."

"Well, see you in class." They ride to the other end of the court.

Steve teases Katy, "You like him. I can tell."

She blushes. "Stop. He's just some boy I go to school with."

They return to shooting hoops. The boys have come up with a new sport, trying to shoot a tennis ball through the basket while riding by. All is peaceful and uneventful.

Vernon Walters, who lives across the street from the park, is watching through his window. He opens it, shouting, "Hey, you kids! You're not supposed to be riding bikes on the basketball court!"

Looking around, Steve responds, "Where did you read that? There aren't any signs."

This won't do for Vernon. "The court is not for bicycles!"

"Come on. They're not bothering anybody."

Vernon snaps, "Mind your own fucking business."

Now Steve gets angry. "Watch that talk! I don't appreciate you using that language in front of my daughter."

Vernon is defiant. "I'll use any kind of damn language I want. Don't be telling me how to talk."

Steve doesn't respond to this, figuring the guy's some old crank. Sometimes it's better not to even bother.

Vernon slams the window shut. Unfortunately, he's more than just an old crank. He's an old crank with a gun. He reaches into a drawer and pulls out a revolver. Then he goes marching outside, straight toward the basketball court, waving it for all to see.

Spotting this, Steve jumps between Vernon and his daughter. The two boys take off. Steve tells Katy to run away. She stays, frozen in fear.

Vernon comes closer. "I told you—no bicycles. Don't argue with me."

Steve tries to maintain his cool. "Look, mister. We don't want any trouble. There's no need for that gun. We're unarmed."

Katy steps in front of her father. Vernon continues to approach, pointing his pistol right at them. He's still spitting out invective.

"Fuck you. You don't tell me *nothing*. I'm the one with the gun."

"Don't point that at my daughter."

"I'll point this thing wherever I damn well please."

Steve, fearing for Katy's safety, reaches for the revolver. In the ensuing struggle, it goes off. Steve falls to the pavement as Katy screams in terror. He had gone through the utter hell of war, fighting to make it back home alive. Yet he leaves his mortal coil in a state of utter bewilderment, unable to comprehend how someone could take it all away so quickly and easily.

32

VERNON WALTERS

Vernon Walters is sitting at a table in an interrogation room at the police station with his lawyer beside him. Two detectives, Brett Owens and Darnell Roberts, sit across from him. Like too many murderers of late, Vernon doesn't seem to exhibit the slightest bit of remorse. Maybe taking an apologetic stance could appear as an admission of guilt, or perhaps these people don't give a damn about whatever grief they cause. Feelings of guilt are receding by the day in a society that puts special emphasis on the self. These days, everyone seems to act as if their own deeds, no matter how depraved, are excusable and justifiable. We've entered an age of utter lack of responsibility.

Owens is the first to speak. "Congratulations, Mr. Walters. You've just killed a twice-decorated army ranger. I guess you must be proud at accomplishing what Al Qaeda and the Taliban failed to do. You should see if they're doing any recruiting in this area."

His lawyer steps in at this. "Let's try to skip the personal attacks. This army ranger you're referring to was reaching for my client's weapon. My client has a legal permit to carry it, and he has the right to stand his ground."

Detective Roberts, who has been studying the police report, feels it might be proper to supply some conveniently omitted details from the defense attorney's version of events. "Mr. Walters, witnesses say you left your home and approached Mr. Colson to confront him. It looks like you left your ground to stand on somebody else's ground, or do you think you own all the ground in town?"

Vernon responds, "Well, he—"

His lawyer cuts him off. "My client can leave his dwelling any time, and he has a right to carry a firearm anywhere he wants. That's the law in this state."

Detective Owens is having none of this. "If you think I'm going to just let your client walk out of here after shooting an unarmed vet with two bronze stars—"

Roberts cuts him off, motioning for them to leave the room. They move out into the hallway.

Roberts says, "Multiple witnesses, including the man's own daughter, have stated that Mr. Colson grabbed Mr. Walters' gun."

Owens asks the obvious. "What if he was doing it to protect her? That would be a perfectly natural response."

"I agree, but it doesn't matter. He reached for the weapon. His lawyer will make mincemeat out of us in court over that. If you're armed, you have the right to stand your ground under the law."

Owens is incredulous. "Now the unarmed guy can't stand his ground? Do these special rights only apply to someone with a gun? Couldn't you as easily argue that Mr. Colson was standing his ground?"

"Of course. I'm sure he was, and I'd swear to that in court. It still won't make any difference."

"So if both guys are standing their ground, whose ground is it?"

"I guess the ground belongs to whoever's left to do the talking."

Owens slams his fist into the wall. "What a fucked-up

law! This is what it's come to? Who the fuck writes these god-damn laws?"

33

UCON

The United Conservative Operative Network, known as UCON, occupies a prominent location on K Street in Washington, DC. UCON exists as a political front for ultra-wealthy donors, along with gun manufacturers, who use this organization to peddle their right-wing agenda behind the scenes. They deploy their financial incentive to not only influence the people's representatives at the federal and state level, but also author legislation pushed by them. They hand the lawmakers a script. This is truly a full-service operation.

Eric Stahlnik, the chief liaison of the organization, sits behind a grand mahogany desk. He has the quiet confidence of one who controls a large, successful corporation. That corporation, which he runs with an iron fist, is the US Congress.

The two men sitting across from him represent K Street. They are former Alabama Congressman Ben Fredrickson and former Florida Congressman Stan Wilberton. As congressional lobbyists, their main function is to siphon money and influence into the right pockets. Due to gerrymandering, too few in Washington feel any sense of responsibility to the voters who put them there. Their primary service is to whomever hands them the biggest pile of cash. If they don't do as they're told, then the pile will instead go to their opponent. We can credit Citizens United for that one. Thanks a lot, Supreme Court! If only our well-meaning forefathers could see what they've wrought, they might have passed a different amendment.

After the perfunctory handshakes and greetings, Eric gets down to business. His two foot soldiers wait at the ready.

"We've pushed the 'stand your ground' laws in Florida and a handful of other states so far. This is a good start, but it's not enough. Our people want us to act in all fifty."

By "our people," he's referring to the conglomerates and investment funds that own the arms manufacturing companies. They have little overall interest in public safety, but make a fortune off public menace.

Ben, the senior of the two lobbyists, cuts to the essence. "We'll get there, but it'll take time, and a good chunk of change."

Eric doesn't flinch. "The firearm companies have deep resources. They've given us the power to line the right pockets and push around anyone who refuses to come onboard. Your job is to do the lining and the pushing."

Stan has also grasped the essence of modern government. "With enough money and intimidation, you can run the whole damn country."

They all chuckle at the mere mention of the obvious. Ben continues. "Just so we understand each other: we'll need a blank check for this one."

Eric agrees. "That won't be a problem. Never has. Never will. Our benefactors possess enough money to buy Congress, if not the White House, which is our ultimate goal."

That's good for another chuckle from this smarmy bunch. He turns to further lines of attack. "We want you to keep up the fight against any attempt to outlaw backdoor gun sales. We find that when more guns fall into the hands of criminals, more law-abiding citizens get the incentive to buy their own. After all, they must protect themselves from these criminals we help arm. Law-abiding citizens also need to protect themselves from one another."

The three again crack up at that last comment. At least *they* find it funny.

Eric explains the larger picture. "Spreading fear has become its own industry. It's resulted in enormous profits for our people. Concealed carry has been a huge moneymaker, and 'stand your ground' will make us even richer. So you keep pushing the laws and talking points we write for you, and we'll keep you well compensated."

Ben nods in appreciation. "You know we can always be counted on to get those little gremlins in Congress and statehouses all over the country marching to our tune."

Eric knows and expects this. "There's never been a shortage of power seekers willing to whore themselves out just to stay in office. I guess that works out to our benefit."

Stan has the last word. "Politics is the world's oldest profession."

Ben adds, "Yeah, but it gives street walkers a bad name."

More laughs. These guys really find one another quite entertaining at our expense.

34

THE COLSON FAMILY

Andrea Colson, wife of the late Steve, is sitting with their daughter, hugging her as family members make condolences. Steve's brother Mike, an attorney, is there with her.

She asks Katy, "Honey, would you sit with your cousins? I want to talk with your uncle."

She refuses to let go of her mother, holding her for a long time before disappearing into the next room.

Andrea tells Mike, "Your brother was a good man. He was trying to protect Katy from this crazy guy with a gun, doing the right thing, reacting the way they trained him."

"You can't be too insane to get a weapon anymore. Anyone who's too scared to leave their house without one already has something wrong with them."

"What kind of world is this? What have we become? This angry nut can take a handgun and threaten people with it, and we're at his mercy! He kills my Steven, who wasn't armed, who loved everybody, who would never hurt an innocent being. He shoots him in cold blood, and then gets to walk away from the whole thing, just because he says he was afraid?"

Mike nods in agreement. "Now you can shoot anyone you want, tell the police you felt threatened, and they send you home, just like that! In all my years as a defense attorney, I would have never expected my clients to get off so easy. This 'stand your ground' law is making a mockery of the justice system."

Andrea, who's been maintaining her composure, breaks down. Mike tries to console her. "I know you're upset. You need to relax."

"You're damn right I am, and no, I will not relax! That's how we've gotten here. Everyone's too relaxed while these gun people walk over the rest of us. I won't relax until this monster that killed my husband gets locked up."

Although this may not be the best time to do so, Mike resorts to dispassionate legal introspection. "Well, Andrea, I don't want you to raise your hopes about getting this guy behind bars."

"Why shouldn't I expect justice? How could that be asking too much?"

"I talked to the prosecutor about this case. I've dealt with him, and he's as tough as they come. However, I need to warn you that this 'stand your ground' law might end up tying his hands."

She finds this excuse unacceptable. "How do they even pass these laws? Who thinks this is a good idea?"

"Nobody does. The politicians who pass these laws either get bought off or threatened by those who generate a fortune selling guns."

Andrea is crestfallen. "This is what it's all about, isn't it? We allow a few pigs to get rich off of the misery of others."

"It's tough to understand. We live in a world full of contradictions. We lock people up when they're caught with a couple of joints, but let them shoot someone and walk away free."

Andrea shakes her head. "The clowns who pass these laws must know they're getting innocent people killed. How could they not?"

"I'm sure they do. They hope and pray it's somebody else's loved one that gets shot instead of their own. As long as it's someone else's family getting destroyed, the politicians that allow this stuff to happen can avoid the issue. They're whistling past the graveyard."

Andrea steels her resolve. "Well, I won't let my husband's murder be in vain. People will find out, whatever it takes. If I have to shout it from the mountaintop, I'll make the public aware this stupid law isn't being used to protect the innocent. It's being used to protect the guilty. This is nothing more than a goddamn license to kill!"

35

JIM TAKES A DARE

It's another weekday in talk-radio land. Jim Savage is a special guest on *The Ted Hunter Show*. After the usual perfunctory comments, followed by a generous dose of ass kissing by Ted on his willing recipient, the two get down to business. Their business is to whine full time about Barack Obama. As Mr. Obama sports a skin color that is anathema to most of both Ted and Jim's audience, there's no shortage of bile flowing out from the transmitter. It's also oozing back through the phone lines.

Jim is peeved about the president's willingness to deny all of the fun-loving patriots the opportunity to further stock up on their beloved assault weapons. Mere revolvers are for sissies, or Clint Eastwood. Obama might even propose a ban on high-capacity ammunition magazines. Since *Rolling Stone* has shunned Jim, this is the only type of magazine that hasn't rejected him. Therefore, it's personal. He thus professes his fondness for the president: "This man, this aberration, this abomination, this lousy piece of human filth, can go suck on my machine gun!"

From the tone of Jim's voice, his gun may be the only appendage of his that's still functional. Ted, who projects similar shortcomings, encourages him to press further. Since Jim has received a visit from the Secret Service regarding his implied threats to the president, he refrains from making further references. Leave that to the callers. Under the cloak of anonymity, they'll be glad to pick up the slack.

The host welcomes them to what passes in his world for a discussion. "William from Portland, you're on the air."

"Hey, Ted. Hey, Jim. I'd like to say you are a couple of great Americans. If it weren't for you guys fighting the good fight, we'd all be through as a nation. These damn commies that have taken over our government will do anything in their power to grab our guns and take away our freedoms. I'll shoot anybody that tries to confiscate one of my guns. In fact, they'll have to pull a semi up to the back door, because I've got a whole bunch of them. Nobody's gonna break into my place, not even a SWAT team. With that guy in the White House, I'm so afraid they're gonna take away my freedom, I can't even leave home."

"Thank you, William. You've made a good point. The only way to be sure they won't get hold of your constitutionally protected arsenal is to stay at home guarding it."

Jim pipes in, "Amen to that, brother."

"Louis from Biloxi, welcome to *The Ted Hunter Show*. What say you?"

"I'll tell you something, the first thing these government thugs will do is try to take away our concealed-carry licenses. They want to take away our God-given rights. I was reading how some lady in Florida a few months ago pulled out her gun and shot a purse snatcher in the back. I guess he didn't get very far. They say she had a winning lottery ticket in there. If this guy had gotten away, he would have been able to cash it in and no doubt would have kept the fifteen bucks for himself."

"Thank you, Louis. This is just another example of how concealed carry, especially the 'stand your ground' law, has changed the face of this great nation. Russ from Denver, you're on the air."

"Thanks for taking my call, Ted. I know you guys don't want to hear this, but there's as good a chance of getting struck by lightning as legally shooting someone with your concealed weapon."

As expected, the mavens of radio pounce on this statement, responding with loud groans. Ted doesn't take well to factual information. "Oh, yeah? Where did you get this nonsense from?"

Russ has come prepared. "All you need to do is check the available Justice Department crime records and cross-check them with government data on lightning strikes. The reason Mr. Savage and his buddies from United Gun Owners don't want you to know these statistics is because it would cut into their revenue. This is how they make their money. I'll bet Savage even makes more off gun sales than record sales."

Jim is getting steamed. "You should try saying that to my face."

Russ from Denver sounds like he'd be glad to take him up on the offer. "Speaking of your face, my wife and I bought tickets to see your ugly mug in concert last year. Since you're so big on concealed carry, how come no one could bring a gun into the venue? Everybody got a pat down. Why do you care so much about our being able to carry a piece anywhere we want, except around *you*? What the hell makes you so special?"

Jim, stumbling in his response, comes up with a fallback excuse. "That decision is up to the promoters."

"That's funny. I'm not aware of any venue that allows the concertgoers to bring in weapons. It's treated just like pro sports. They don't allow firearms in stadiums, either. You're so gung ho about everybody being free to carry wherever they want. As a UGO board member, why don't you refuse to play any concert hall that won't let your adoring fans take guns with them?"

"Look, buddy, no one's making you come to one of my concerts."

"Actually, it was my wife that wanted to go. If it was up to me, I would prefer to listen to chalk scratching on a blackboard, which I'd equate to listening to your vocals."

"I don't need to deal with this kind of abuse."

"Hey, man. I was just messing with you. Tell you what: Here's my challenge to you, Jim. How about you put your money where your mouth is and go on tour playing only at venues that allow the fans to carry weapons? Show us all how safe it will be. Come on, man. You're a high-profile gun guy. This is your big chance to make a statement and prove a point. If it's safe enough for you to be surrounded by strangers with guns, then it should be safe enough for the rest of us."

Jim is doing his level best not to get baited into a corner. "Well, I'll discuss this with my manager and see what he says."

"Sure you will. We can hardly wait. Personally, I don't believe you've got the guts to do it. You should prove to us all you're not the coward I think you are."

Ted cuts off the call. "We've heard enough from this moron. I'm sure our Second Amendment freedoms needn't extend to rock concerts. Just imagine the insurance costs."

Unfortunately for the host and his guest, other callers are waiting in the wings, ready to rub it in further. One after another, they smoke out Jim for his hypocrisy, daring him to take up the challenge.

"That dude was right. You should lead by example. Why don't you trust your own audience?"

"What's good for the goose is good for the gander. If

you insist that the rest of us will be fine walking around with armed citizens whenever we set foot in public, then it should be OK for you, too."

"You haven't got the guts, Savage! I'm putting a recording of this show on the Internet, and it's going to go viral. Everyone's gonna know you backed down. The whole world's about to find out you're a phony and a wuss."

Jim's had enough. Finally losing his cool, he broadcasts to the world he'll only play venues on his upcoming tour that will allow the audience to carry firearms. Once the radio show is over, Jim finds himself weighed down by more than a tinge of remorse. In fact, he's already thinking of ways to back down from this challenge, even if he has to cancel every concert.

36

RANDY REARMS

The Steeles are spending another quiet evening at home, which to them has become both a fortress and a jail. They've pulled the shades tight, shutting off the outside world. A ringing telephone serves as a reminder the outside world won't leave them alone. Nancy picks it up. After listening for a second, she hangs up, looking shaken.

Randy asks, "Who was it?"

"It was another death threat."

He snaps, "Our goddamn number's supposed to be unlisted! How the hell are they getting it?"

"Cathy tells me a blogger somehow got hold of it and put it out on the Internet."

"I'd like to shoot that fucking blogger, too."

Nancy is at her wits' end. "You should see the horrible stuff people are posting online. It's making me too scared to step out of the house."

"I told you to stay off the goddamn computer. That thing's cost me a fortune. How come you gotta buy a new dress off eBay every other day? I'm gonna throw the fucking thing out the goddamn window!"

Now the worst dawns on Nancy. "If they put our phone number online, they're gonna find our address, too. I'll bet somebody will try to kill us."

"Yeah, well, thanks to you, we can't even defend ourselves. Why'd you tell the detectives how many guns I've got? Huh? They came and took every fucking one of them."

"You know a condition of your bail is you can't keep a gun in the house until the trial is over."

"So what? I could have given them one goddamn gun. Why'd you tell them about the other four? How the hell are we supposed to protect ourselves?"

"Maybe we should hire private security."

"Oh yeah. Who's gonna pay for it?"

"What about the money people donated for your defense? Couldn't we use some for our protection?"

"Nice try. Once our fucking crook lawyer found out how much was in the account, his bills magically inflated."

"Really?"

He maintains his defiance. "In this country, you're supposed to be innocent until proven guilty. They can't take our guns away."

"Well, they did."

This doesn't sit right with Randy. "The hell with it. Screw the damn court. Here's what you're gonna do. Tomorrow, first thing, you go out and buy another gun. You just put the thing in your name. In fact, I want you to get two guns. You're gonna carry one, too, when you leave the house for groceries."

Nancy looks shocked. "I will not carry a gun. I wish we had no guns at all. What good have they done for us?"

"They help me sleep at night. That's what they do for us. You think I'll let some spook just walk in the kitchen and make himself a sandwich while we're upstairs sleeping? Screw it! You're gonna buy two goddamn guns tomorrow, one for you and one for me."

"I don't have a permit."

"Fuck the damn permit! You're not leaving the house

without a goddamn piece. You understand? Tomorrow! Be-sides, we need to stock up on weapons before they try to pass that stupid restriction on buying only one gun a month. Can you believe that shit? One gun a month! How the hell's some-body supposed to protect themselves?"

37

MAGGIE O'ROURKE

Maggie O'Rourke is an award-winning investigative journalist for the *Orlando Tribune*. She has earned a reputation for being tough, honest, and fair. She has interviewed many hard cases in her career and never shies away from asking someone a question, welcome or otherwise.

Today, she sits across a desk from her editor, William Kohler. He has complete respect for her abilities, coming through time and again on assignments.

"How are you, Maggie?"

"Other than feeling tired from staying up late doing research, I'm doing OK."

He chuckles. "Though school's well in the rearview mirror, homework is forever."

"I like to be thorough."

"I know you do. It's why you're my number one. You did a terrific job with your series of columns on domestic violence. It opened a lot of eyes, gotten all kinds of positive feedback."

"I feel strongly about this. It seems to get glossed over too often. People want to look the other way. It's amazing how many women accept it as normal behavior, conditioned to blame themselves until they realize they're not alone."

"I've got a new assignment for you. I'm sure you're aware of the recent Rogers shooting. You remember that unarmed fifteen-year-old kid? Well, it appears the police let his killer walk under the 'stand your ground' defense, or I should say, 'stand your ground' excuse. His parents haven't accepted that decision and have hired Stanley Weisman to represent them."

Maggie is aware of who he is, and it surprises her to hear the victim's family would bring in such a high-profile trial attorney. A former prosecutor, he's an expert at making waves.

William continues. "He's brought this case to the national media. It's breaking in a big way. The focus is the 'stand your ground' law, which is what he intends to put the spotlight on. He's also fighting for the police to bring murder charges against the shooter. It looks like the state may go over the heads of the locals and bring in a special prosecutor. I know you're close to some folks in the attorney general's office and hope you can dig up inside info."

Maggie is eager for the assignment. She believes this 'stand your ground' nonsense has been a catastrophe waiting to happen. "I'll tell you what, Bill. I'm interested in digging a lot deeper on this whole thing and plan on finding out who's been behind pushing this law on us."

"You have our full resources. Good luck."

She thanks him and is out the door in a flash, ready to dive into her assignment.

As the drive to the state Department of Justice in Tallahassee will take up most of her day, Maggie phones ahead to someone she knows within the institution. The staff sets aside a large stack of records as they await her arrival.

Her friend, Thelma Lewis, guides her to a small anteroom where she can peruse the material in private. In that room is also a copy machine stocked with plenty of blank paper. For the next three hours, Maggie goes through one report after another. It's past nightfall when she heads back to Orlando with a car full of crime reports.

Over the following couple of weeks, she culls a sizeable number of cases where the 'stand your ground' defense was used in Florida alone. Most were dismissed without a trial or any plea bargain. Many of these incidents transpired within a short distance of Orlando, as it sits near the middle of the state. The proximity will give Maggie ample opportunity to interview both the victims' families and those of the perpetrators. One thing she excels at is getting people to talk, even those still shocked and stricken by grief.

Maggie's first stop after returning is her editor's office. He is eager to find out what sort of state records she has been able to recover. They also have a few novel ideas to consider.

"Bill, after thinking about this, I believe we should focus on the extremism ingrained in the American gun culture. Sometimes, the best way to argue is to smoke out the other side, baiting them into making the argument for you. I've put in a call to Congresswoman Sheila Lehnahan's office, and I think we might get her involved. The idea is to plant a poison pill."

"What do you mean by that?"

"Well, it would involve the blowup technique. One of the most effective ways to undermine a disagreement is to agree with your opponent while amplifying the absurdity of their argument."

This intrigues Bill. "I'm all ears."

"You know how the pro-gun forces are always leaning on the Second Amendment? They carry on as if it nullifies every statute they don't like, which means *all* gun laws in existence."

"They're intractable on that. It's used to shut down any discussion having anything to do with restricting firearm access."

"Well, the gun lobby minions are getting bold in their insistence that the only answer to the problem of gun violence is more guns. The argument they make is that the solution should only involve denying firearms to violent criminals and the insane. However, the Constitution, which they always love to bring up, makes no special distinction concerning the rights of ex-cons or the mentally ill. Why do we single out and compromise the Second Amendment just for these individuals? The First Amendment, along with every other, protects felons. How can we deny them the full protection of only the Second Amendment?"

"I see your point, Maggie, but where are you going with this?"

"If we could get someone in Congress to propose overturning the law barring these prohibitions from owning firearms, we could back the pro-gun forces into a corner. It would force them to come out against this bill, which would be a tacit endorsement of gun control. It may lead to further concessions for the sake of sanity."

William won't quite allow her to indulge that fantasy. "It explains why they resist any change. It all plays into their 'slippery slope' argument. It's a novel idea, Maggie, I'll give you credit for that. Although a bill like this would have such a poor chance of passing even Sheila wouldn't touch it, that doesn't stop us from editorializing about it. The more I consider it, the better it sounds. This is an excellent concept to develop into a series of articles. Why not work it into your investigation of the 'stand your ground' laws?"

Maggie appreciates this input. William has always supported her. He's never short of good ideas, either. "If you're willing to devote enough space in the paper, maybe we ought to present a primer on the Constitution itself. I'm sure most of the public hasn't bothered to read the thing, aside from quoting only a few select parts."

William likes the idea. Too few newspapers bother to educate their readers anymore. "We'll publish this as soon as possible and post the entire text of the document online. Following that, I'd like to run your series, with special emphasis on how the Second Amendment is being used to provide cover for the passage of these ridiculous laws. Congress might be reluctant to act. However, sometimes any eventual actions taken on their part begin with an initial prodding of the public. As usual, it's our job to prod."

Maggie is lucky to have an editor who's so supportive. Such hasn't always been the case. Too many of the newer ones coming up have an inordinate fear of offending someone. William harkens back to the old-school, Ben Bradlee type.

"How's your research advancing on the Marvin Rogers shooting?"

"We're turning up lots of illuminating evidence."

"I want to expand this investigation into a detailed examination of every case where the 'stand your ground' defense has been used. We should assemble a perspective on how this has affected things in the state during its first five years of implementation. I'd like you to interview as many of the victims' families as you can."

"I'm on it. My staff is pulling up records. Since this law has been in place, we've seen the number of homicides ruled justifiable triple in Florida. By justifiable, that just means the prosecutor wasn't able to bring charges. It still doesn't mean these murders were justified in the true sense of the word."

"Well put. Let's get the real facts. In some cases, this will involve digging further than the police investigators were willing to go. Too often, they act like it's not worth the bother."

"You know how some prosecutors prefer to just focus on the slam dunks."

"This is where we come in. What did you find at the state hall of records?"

"We've uncovered a lot, and the results so far have been shocking. Rather than finding that 'stand your ground' protects people from criminals, we're discovering the exact opposite. We see a pattern of murders where this law has in more and more cases protected the perpetrators at the fatal expense of the innocent."

"That doesn't surprise me. Everyone should have seen that coming."

"Under the enacted laws, a criminal without a felony rap can get a permit to carry a gun. He could take it to a crime scene, use it on a law-abiding victim, then argue he was using it to protect himself from bodily harm."

Bill understands the picture. "So if you try to defend yourself against a predator, they may now shoot you and claim self-defense."

"Incredible, isn't it? The results should have been obvious. I'll want a full staff on this, all the resources you can muster."

"You'll get whatever help you need. This is a big project, which is why I assigned it to you, Maggie. You're the best one for the job."

They're interrupted by a knock on the door. It's Maggie's assistant, Joel Mulhern.

"Sorry to interrupt, but I've gotten those records you requested. You won't believe this. We got word they've dropped charges against the guy who shot that unarmed vet on the basketball court."

This news stuns William. "No plea? They threw the whole thing out?"

"Correct. This comes straight from the DA's office."

"Thanks, Joel."

William waits for him to leave the room, then turns his attention back to Maggie. "Give the man's family some time to grieve, then see if you can talk with his wife."

"That won't be necessary. She contacted me first. She's pretty fired up about this, wants to form a victim's support group and everything."

"This 'stand your ground' law has opened a huge hole in the justice system. It's created a condition where you could start an altercation and still legally shoot the other guy if things aren't going your way."

She takes his argument further. "It doesn't matter who's winning the fight. Regardless, if you only say you feared for your life, you can get away with murder. The victim doesn't even need to be armed, just permanently unavailable for counter testimony."

William looks as determined as ever. He likes being involved in a worthwhile mission.

"As long as the state legislature won't do anything about it, we're the last line of defense. If we don't speak on behalf of the victims, no one will. I'm telling you, this country's sure going to hell."

Now it's Maggie who's offering reassurance. "Not if we can help it."

38

MAGGIE AND NANCY

As Maggie approaches the Steele house, she spots a late-model SUV pulling out of the driveway with a female behind the wheel. Assuming this to be Mrs. Steele, the reporter takes advantage of the opportunity to speak with her alone, away from her husband. She follows the car until it pulls into a parking lot. The driver walks into a store as Maggie parks nearby, waiting for her return.

A short time later, Nancy Steele comes out carrying a bag of groceries. As she's putting them in the trunk, Maggie approaches her.

"Excuse me. Are you Mrs. Steele?"

This catches Nancy by surprise. "Who are you?"

"I'm Maggie O'Rourke from the *Orlando Tribune.*"

Nancy puts up her guard. "Oh no. I'm not supposed to be talking to anybody."

"Don't worry, I understand. You can trust me."

"I can't. If my husband ever found out I was speaking to you, he'd kill me."

"Are you afraid of him?"

"What do you think?"

"You shouldn't have to fear him. It's no way to live. Please, let me buy you a cup of coffee. We'll talk about anything you want. OK?"

Nancy hesitates, considering the offer. Her resistance

softens.

"I liked your series on battered women. After I read that, I wanted to thank you in person. So I guess the least I could do is join you for coffee, but please don't get me in trouble."

"I promise I won't."

They walk to a bistro next to the grocery store. These days, it's easier to find a coffee house than a gas station.

Maggie tries to put her at ease. "I like your dress."

"Thanks. This is just something I wear sometimes. I found a good deal for it on eBay."

"Hey, a bargain's a bargain."

They share a laugh. Maggie finds that the best interviews start with unrelated small talk.

Maggie orders black, while Nancy goes for the latte. They grab a corner table, out of earshot from the other patrons.

Maggie asks, "How do you like their coffee?"

"It's excellent, delicious."

"This place has the finest in town."

They sip in silence for a while. Maggie decides to steer the conversation toward something more substantive. "Mrs. Steele…"

"Nancy. Call me Nancy."

"Sure. Nancy, you mentioned that you liked my series on battered women. Do you consider yourself to be one?"

"I don't think I should talk about this."

This is the point where Maggie, being foremost an investigative reporter, sometimes makes promises that may not always be kept.

"What you and I discuss regarding your personal life will remain private. I'm not recording this or taking notes. I promise never to write about anything you say without your permission. You have my word."

This puts her subject somewhat at ease, which is the whole reason for giving such questionable assurances.

"Look, my husband Randy isn't a bad man. I mean, he has a temper, but…"

"Has he ever hit you?"

Nancy hesitates to answer, even though Maggie is just asking for confirmation of the obvious.

"There have been times, but they weren't his fault. Sometimes I say the wrong thing, and it sets him off. I need to be more careful."

"That's no excuse. Neither he, nor anyone else, may strike you for any reason."

"Well, he doesn't mean to do it. You know how men can be."

"No, Nancy, real men don't act that way. They don't hit women, and they don't make them live in fear."

Now Nancy is feeling self-conscious. "I think I've already said too much. I need to pick up a couple more things, and if I'm gone too long, Randy will go ballistic. You understand?"

"Sure, I understand."

Now nervous, she gets up to depart. "It's been nice meeting you. Thanks for the coffee."

"It's been nice meeting you, too. We'll speak again when you have more time."

Not if Nancy can help it. "OK. Sorry, I need to leave."

She scurries away.

39

JOE'S LIFE ONLINE

It's a weekday afternoon. Joe Stupnik has taken the day off. He's indulging in his favorite activity: sitting at his computer, watching Internet porn, talking to the screen, and pointing his gun at it. What a life. Lucky for him, the monitor can't talk back.

He mutters away. "That's right, bitch. How'd you like that cold hard steel stuck up inside you? You like that? You want more? I'll give you more. You'll be begging me for mercy, bitch."

The doorbell rings. Startled, Joe yanks the computer plug out of the wall. He goes to the window, pulling back the drapes to peer outside. A female stands at the front door. It's Maggie O'Rourke. He opens the door part way, with the chain still attached. Joe asks, "What do you want?"

"Are you Joe Stupnik?"

"Who are you?"

"I'm Maggie O'Rourke from the *Orlando Tribune*. Are you Joe?"

"I might be. Why do you ask?"

"I would like to speak with you. May I come in?"

He peers outside, looking around with suspicion. "Is anyone else here with you?"

"No, I'm alone."

"Why do you want to talk?"

"I hear you had an incident where you were forced to defend yourself."

"I have nothing to say to you." Joe tries to close the door.

Now Maggie lays on the butter. "No, wait. We're doing an article about how the 'stand your ground' law has helped save lives, about how heroic your actions were."

Joe's mood brightens. He takes the chain off the door. "Come in."

"Thank you. I promise I won't take too much of your time."

They stand in the vestibule in awkward silence. Maggie senses that Joe isn't used to having female company, or any company. She puts on her most soothing voice. "Could we sit down?"

He appears flustered, uneasy around an actual live woman. "Oh sure. Right this way. Make yourself at home."

He sits on the couch. She takes a chair to the side. Now he becomes more eager. "You're doing a profile on me?"

"Um, yes. It will be part of a larger story on gun owners who exercised their Second Amendment rights."

"Hey, you can't beat the Second Amendment. I'm all for that. If it weren't for the Second Amendment, there wouldn't be a First Amendment."

"Why is that, Joe? Do you believe people aren't free to speak unless they have a gun to protect themselves?"

"Well, I guess so, sometimes. I mean, armed militias protect our right to free speech. It's our last line of defense against an oppressive government."

"Do you think our government is oppressive?"

"Oh sure. They're trying to shove taxes, health care, and other oppressive laws down our throats."

"So you feel citizens should arm themselves against

the government?"

"Yes, I do. If we have guns, the government won't be able to take them."

Maggie takes a moment to digest that logic. "Do you envision a situation where you would use your gun against a federal agent?"

"If they tried to confiscate my weapons, then I know I would. The Nazis did that. We have a right to bear arms. No one can grab my guns, not even the government. Don't you agree?"

Maggie attempts to be diplomatic in the face of such staunch certitude. "I believe we have certain rights under the Constitution, yes."

"We sure do."

Having had enough of the typical, repetitive pro-gun rhetoric, she steers the conversation back to Joe's recent brush with infamy. "Please tell me what happened to you in the bar the night of the shooting. Were you being threatened?"

"You bet I was. I was just minding my own business, and this big guy started picking on me. I had to defend myself. It was him or me."

"He picked a fight with you for no reason at all?"

"That's right, and he was twice my size. It's why I carry a gun. I'm not so big. Guys like me get pushed around sometimes. I don't care to put up with that. Since I carry a firearm—legally, I might add—nobody will get away with pushing me around."

"I saw the police report. Witnesses said you started the fight."

He gets angry. "That's not true! This was in a crowded bar. How do they know what happened? They have no idea! The law says I'm allowed to defend myself!"

"Of course you can, Joe. I'm not accusing you of doing

anything bad. I want to give you a chance to tell the public your side of the story."

"Good. Some people jump to the wrong conclusions. Hell, they won't even let me go back inside that bar. Maybe I should sue them. They should be glad I was there. If I hadn't stopped this guy, he might have hurt someone else. Who knows what could happen?"

Maggie has gotten the gist of it. She's not here to retry the case, only conduct an interview. Maybe she'll become a prosecutor in the next life. In her line of work, she hears all kinds of whoppers. Joe has provided her with a wheelbarrow full of them.

"Thank you for your time, Joe."

As she gets up to leave, a look of disappointment comes over him. He was just getting warmed up. It's not every day he can find anyone to listen to him.

40

THE ROBINSONS

The Robinsons sit at their kitchen table. There is no conversation, as a heavy shroud has reigned over this couple since losing their daughter. In relation to that, nothing else warrants a single word.

A ringing doorbell breaks their silence. Not expecting or wanting company, Sam walks to the front door, spotting an unfamiliar woman standing on the other side. He opens it, asking, "May I help you?"

"Hello. Are you Sam Robinson?"

"Yes, I am."

"I'm Maggie O'Rourke, a reporter for the *Orlando Tribune*."

There is a flash of recognition. "I know who you are."

"Do you mind if I speak with you?"

"Come in."

Unlike some of the previous encounters on this assignment, she feels welcome. He leads her to a chair in the living room. His wife comes to join him on the couch.

"This is Mary. Mary, this is Maggie O'Rourke from the *Orlando Tribune*."

She gives Maggie a welcoming smile. This is the first moment she has smiled at anyone since the murder of her Angelica.

"It's very nice to meet you, Mary."

"It's nice to meet you, too, Ms. O'Rourke. I've enjoyed reading your columns."

"I'm sure this is a sensitive time for you, and I don't mean to intrude. If you wouldn't mind, I want to please speak with you about your daughter. It's important to tell her story."

This heartens Mary, who's grateful for the opportunity. "Thank you. My Angie was a beautiful child. She got along with everyone."

Sam is also appreciative. "The outside world doesn't care about people like us."

Maggie understands. "Every life is precious. We should all be accorded dignity and respect. Please tell me about your daughter."

Mary speaks first. "My Angelica was a wonderful girl. She was special, a good student, didn't cause trouble, and had a lot of friends. Everyone around here liked her."

"Was it safe for her to walk through the neighborhood?"

Sam bristles at this. "Why shouldn't it be? If the damn police would sweep these bastards off the street, it would be safer for everybody. They don't want to bother. They just drive by and wave at the drug dealers."

"Do you believe they don't care?"

"Either that or they're afraid they might get outgunned. The criminals around here carry firepower that nobody should have. It's like Dodge City up in here."

Maggie aspires to do more than report details about a victim through testimonials from the surviving family members. She avoids the typical TV news reporter's questions, uttered with a microphone shoved in the face of some grieving parent, asking, "How does it make you feel?" She would prefer to ask something more proactive. "What would you like to see done to honor your daughter?"

Sam answers, "I don't want her to have died in vain. People should be made aware that her life was important. We also need to take these damn guns off the street. When I hear these useless politicians say there's nothing they can do, it makes my skin crawl. They keep saying criminals will always be able to find guns. Well, I'd like to find out whom they're getting them from. Those are the real culprits."

41

NANCY GOES SHOPPING

Randy Steele sits on the couch in silence, fidgeting away, when he spots Nancy's car pulling into the driveway. He meets her at the door.

"Did you pick up what I asked?"

"Yes."

"Did you have any problem?"

"None. I don't think these people much care whom they sell their guns to. I walked out of there in ten minutes."

She hands him a box containing two brand-new, identical 9mm Glock handguns.

"Nice. You did well. Did anyone recognize you?"

"I'm sure the clerk at the firearm store recognized me, but he said nothing."

"Yeah. All they want is your money."

"I filled out a form, passed the background check, and I was on my way. He didn't ask me who the second gun was for."

"That's because it's none of his damn business who it's for. They're not even allowed to ask."

"No wonder guns end up in the wrong hands. They couldn't care less what happens once you're out the door."

"Don't worry about it. It's not their concern or yours. You keep one in your purse from now on when you leave the house."

"Are you sure I don't need a permit?"

"Fuck the damn permit. You just take the gun with you."

"I'm not comfortable carrying a gun. Guns scare me."

"Oh yeah? What scares you more, carrying a gun or running into some spook that wants to steal your money?"

"I'd rather give them the money, to tell you the truth. I don't want to kill anybody."

"That's *my* goddamn money! Got that? I worked my ass off for it and I'll be damned if I'm gonna let some scumbag take it from me or you. Violence is all these people understand."

A knock interrupts his rant. Suspicious as always, Randy picks up his new gun as he approaches the door. He cracks it open. There is an unfamiliar-looking female standing outside.

"Who are you?"

"Are you Randy Steele?"

"I asked who the fuck are you?"

"I'm Maggie O'Rourke from the *Orlando Tribune*."

Randy rips off the chain, swinging the door all the way open. "What the hell do you want?"

Although put off by Randy's attitude, Maggie soldiers on. Besides, she has handled tough nuts before and has a history of refusing to back down.

"I'm writing an article about the 'stand your ground' law, and I'd like to offer you the opportunity to make your case to the public."

Nancy is standing in the background, scared and shaking her head at the reporter, mouthing the words, "Go away." As is typical, Randy can never pass up a chance bark at someone, anyone. "I'm allowed to defend myself. I don't need to give excuses to you or anybody else. Besides, I'm not supposed to be talking to people until we win this damned case, so get the hell off my property."

Maggie had been expecting a response like this and only came to the Steele house in an attempt to provoke Randy's temper. From experience, she has found that when some guys fly off the handle, they can blurt out incriminating things. That he's holding a hidden gun in his other hand behind the door might have encouraged her to show greater restraint. Unaware of this, she thus shows him a little additional defiance. "Are you threatening me?"

"It's not a threat. It's an order. I could shoot you under the 'stand your ground' law right now just for trespassing."

Having had more than enough, Nancy snaps, "Randy! Stop it!" She turns to Maggie. "You'd better go. Please!"

Maggie walks away.

Randy is fuming at the intrusion. "That bitch! How the fuck did she find our address?"

"Who knows?"

He focuses his ire on Nancy. "You don't speak to nobody. You hear me? Not her, nobody. If I find out you've spoken to anybody…"

"I won't! I won't!"

Agitated and upset, she runs up the stairs and slams the bedroom door behind her. She feels betrayed by Maggie, terrified her words might show up in the local newspaper.

42

THE MORRIS HOME

Andy Morris lives with his parents in a nondescript suburban subdivision. There are thousands of such developments throughout the country. These neighborhoods are usually peaceful with low crime. The neighbors watch out for one another. Evil rarely intrudes from the outside. However, as is too often the case, danger may lie within.

On a quiet, sunny afternoon, Margaret Morris and her friend Sally are lounging around the backyard next to an aboveground pool. Each is nursing a glass of Chardonnay, sporting sunglasses, and soaking up the rays. Inside the house, Andy is playing hide-and-seek with his younger brother Robbie. Sally's daughter Jenny, who has just turned seven, plays with them. Andy still wears his bandage from the pediatrician's office.

Sally is enjoying lying back on the chaise lounge with her friend. These moments of respite are welcome, allowing her to experience the fleeting feeling of not having a care in the world.

"This is the life, isn't it? We've got sunshine, a glass of wine, and nothing to do."

Margaret begs to differ. "I hate to say it, but I'd like to ship my kids off somewhere for a week or two. I need the break."

"Boys can be a real handful sometimes, and they pretty much stay that way throughout adulthood."

They both chuckle at that.

"You should see them when your daughter's not here. They seem to behave better when Jenny's around. She's a nice girl. You're raising her right."

"Yours are typical boys. I wouldn't worry about it."

"They could use a little more supervision from their father. He needs to spend more time around the house."

"Where is he today?"

"He's off hunting somewhere with his cousin. He should be back later after I've conveniently put them to bed."

"Why should *you* do all the work? They're his kids, too."

"It's fine with me. He'll probably come home drunk anyway."

"Oh."

"Make that drunk and carrying a loaded weapon."

"Well, that's a comforting thought. What could beat alcohol and guns?"

"You never know when he might run into a squirrel with a bad attitude."

They both laugh.

Meanwhile, inside the house, things have quieted down. The two boys are in the kitchen. Andy asks his brother, "Hey, Robbie, want a cookie?"

"Yeah."

"I found out where Mom hides them."

He grabs a chair, using it to climb up on the counter. He opens a cupboard, reaching for the top shelf. There, he sees a jar marked Cookies. He sets it down and opens it. There aren't any cookies inside. However, Andy finds something even more exciting. It's a big, shiny revolver.

"Whoa! Look what I found!"

He pulls it out. As he does so, Jenny walks into the kitchen. Holding the gun, Andy turns toward her. "Hey, Jenny..."

The gun goes off. She cries out and falls to the floor.

The loud bang startles Margaret and Sally. This is a moment where the unthinkable intrudes so profoundly that one gets the desperate urge to grasp backward in time, to the previous second, when all was well.

The two women jump up, running into the house. There is a deathly silence, followed by hysterical screaming coming from inside.

43

JENNY

The surviving members of Jenny's family gather at her house. Sally's best friend Margaret isn't welcome. Although Sally can't allow herself to blame Andy, she is furious at both his parents for leaving him with easy access to the instrument of her daughter's death. Everyone gathered is devastated. Sally sits with her brother Gene in the anteroom.

"Someone's got to pay for this. I don't mean Margaret. That dimwitted husband of hers put it there. They should lock him up."

Gene offers little consolation. "Well, I'd love to see the bastard put away. However, they almost never hold the owners responsible when their kid picks up their gun and shoots somebody. This sounds ridiculous, but it's true."

"Why? What about gun locks? Aren't they supposed to keep their firearms secured?"

"No. They tried to pass a law some years ago that mandated those, but the lobbyists killed it. That's too bad, because it would save a lot of lives, especially those of children."

"Why are these people so untouched? My little girl's dead! Doesn't that mean anything? Who stands up for the victims? Are those in Congress such cowards they can't even lift a finger to protect a child?"

She breaks down. Gene wants to be more comforting, but he's too full of anger. "Our representatives are just a bunch of whores. The gun lobby has paid them off. Do you know they've passed laws giving immunity to the sellers and manufacturers? Unlike all other industries in the United States, these bastards have to answer to nobody. They keep pushing everyone around, always getting their way, striking fear in any politician that dares to stand up to them."

Sally, too, is spitting mad. "They're cowards, every last one of them. We've become a nation of armed cowards."

44

JULIUS STALKER

Maggie comes bursting into William Kohler's office, waving an official report she has received through her connections at the Department of Justice. She doesn't notice the stranger sitting off to the side.

"You won't believe these records. Of over twelve thousand homicides by firearms yearly, fewer than two hundred are ruled justifiable. That goes for the entire United States. Less than one out of every sixty fatal shootings is legal. Shouldn't the people be made aware of this? These are statistics the gun lobby has fought to keep locked away from American citizens. This is public information. The country needs to know the truth."

William doesn't respond. She stops as she notices the stranger in their midst.

"Maggie, this is Julius Stalker. He's from the board of our parent company. Julius, this is Maggie O'Rourke, our senior investigative reporter."

She is uptight at the sight of him. She knows who he is, and she's sure he isn't there to compliment them on what a great job they're doing. She greets him through clenched teeth. "Good to meet you."

Julius doesn't even bother to conceal his contempt. "I've heard so much about you."

At that, he nods to William and leaves the room. Maggie's had warmer greetings from a corpse, most of whom were better looking, too. "Why is he here?"

"He got wind of the story you're working on."

"So? Since when does he involve himself with our content?"

William never stammers like he's doing now. "He, um, he's concerned about balance. He insists we put equal weight on both sides of the issue. We need to show how the 'stand your ground' law is saving lives, too."

"Well, it isn't! They sold the public a big bill of goods. This law only serves the guilty. Since when can he dictate what we write about?"

"Since he's been contacted by lobbyists with UCON. The owners are concerned that certain major advertisers will boycott our paper, those who do a large ancillary business in guns and ammo."

"I thought this was supposed to be a free press! Is this what things have come to? Anytime we might step on someone's toes the board can censure us? Since when do you respond to these kinds of threats?"

"I respond when my job is on the line."

"Whatever happened to your principles? No one's pushed you around before.

"It's more complicated than that. Thanks to cross-ownership and industry consolidation, these media conglomerates become more and more powerful. They're injecting themselves into matters of what gets disseminated and what gets buried, so to speak."

"Maybe we're missing the real story. This is what we should write about. The public needs to see the larger picture. This is no time to pull back."

"In a perfect world, yes. However, in this world, we're stymied. These companies have the power to not only fire you, but lock you out of the industry altogether. There'd be nowhere else to go. We'd be lucky to get hired at the local free press."

"Well, that's so comforting to know."

"No one is saying we can't publish your articles. We need to take opposing viewpoints into account."

"This false equivalency is ruining the country. It's like, for every argument, we need to find an equal and opposite position, no matter how ludicrous. If we write about the toxicity of pollution, we must balance it with the story that pollution creates jobs. If we run an interview with Nelson Mandela, we also have to publish an article featuring David Duke. The right wing is taking us down the sewer. When will it be enough?"

"Well, at some point we still need to answer to whoever's paying the bills."

She fixes him with a steely gaze. "There's a term for that. It's called prostitution."

45

DRINKS FOR TWO

Maggie is sitting at a table in an upscale, downtown bar. A friend and colleague, Janet Myers, joins her. Although Maggie has been silent about her current assignment, she needs to spill. Janet always provides a sympathetic ear.

"This whole project is turning into a nightmare. It's not just the details, but also the larger picture. Now I need to check first with the higher-ups to make sure my subject fits the ideology of whoever currently owns the newspaper."

Although her response isn't comforting, Janet says, "Welcome to the real world."

"This world is becoming less real."

"The old days are gone. Yesterday's rules no longer apply. As these media conglomerates become larger and more powerful, the individual voices become smaller."

"You'd think the one place to still allow free speech would be newspapers, but that's not the case."

"Sure. Look at the Dixie Chicks. Remember when they had the nerve to criticize George W. Bush? They were banished from radio overnight. Yet when a clown like Jim Savage goes off on Obama, he not only gets to stay on the airwaves, but also treated as royalty over at *Right-Wing News*. Hell, he's got Lou Hennesy's lipstick smeared all over his ass."

"I guess we know which side's running the networks. They've taken advantage of deregulation and consolidation."

"It will only turn worse. You'll see. The public acts like a bunch of sheep. They're sleepwalking through life and don't want to be disturbed. This article you're working on is something most people won't care about until it affects someone in their own family."

"Yet they still feel powerless to do anything about it. In my research, we're finding a surprising percentage of families have lost either a friend or a relative to gun violence, and the stories are always the same. Criminals rarely kill these victims. Most of the time it's about someone losing his or her temper with somebody else over something stupid."

"That's it. They'll sell a handgun to anybody and give him or her a license to carry it anywhere they want. Are all of them mature or sane enough to handle the responsibility? You know, even the police have to get checked for mental competency before they can carry a gun. Do you think they check the competency of every civilian who applies for permit? Hell no."

"So we've got a bunch of half-cocked people running around half-cocked."

They both snicker at that one.

"Yeah. So what's the solution? I'll tell you what it is. They end up pushing everyone to carry a gun to protect himself or herself from *everybody else* who carries one. The criminals, who these deluded assholes thought would be intimidated by this concealed-carry nonsense, are sitting on the sidelines. They're laughing while they watch a bunch of so-called law-abiding idiots shoot each other. People don't need protection from criminals. They need protection from themselves."

"This is the problem. We're stuck with a political class that's risen to power not by appealing to people's sensibilities but rather to their emotions. Stirring up hatred and fear stirs up votes. This results in a Congress that runs by serving the hateful and the fearful. They stay in power by shoveling out more hate and more fear. We have to attack this country and that country. We all need to carry a firearm. If we could only eliminate everyone that makes us nervous, we'd all be so happy."

"Just tell one of these gun crazies that the true source of their problems lies within. These folks aren't real big on psychological self-examination. Try to point out to someone who's overwhelmed with paranoia that there's nothing to fear but fear itself. We're now stuck with a government that undermines itself by catering to the most hysterical voices out there."

"That's because this country isn't run on brains, but on emotion."

"Emotion without brains equals armed and clueless."

46

R.T. DAILEY

The morning sun streams through the bedroom window of Robert Thomas Dailey, known as R.T. by his few friends. Indistinguishable from millions of other high school seniors, he's quiet, keeping to himself. As his alarm goes off, he shakes off the last vestiges of sleep and begins preparations for another day of classes.

For no outward reason, he appears to be in an especially good mood, whistling a happy tune as he gets dressed. He fires up his computer, checking his favorite Internet forums for the latest useless patter. As he has received little e-mail correspondence from anyone he knows as of late, R.T. has chosen to remove the spam filter just to hear something from somebody. This means his inbox is full of pitches for male-enhancement products. However, today, he shows an interest in a different form of male enhancement.

As both his parents are at work, he makes his own breakfast. It's not too difficult filling a bowl of cereal with milk. He eats in silence, staring at the side of his neighbor's house, which is all you can spot from any kitchen window in the neighborhood. After rinsing out the bowl and putting it in the dishwasher, R.T. puts on a light jacket and backpack. There is just one more thing he needs to pack: a handgun from the nightstand drawer in his parents' bedroom.

He rides his bike to school, waving to neighbors along

the way. The street is a patchwork of trimmed lawns and aluminum siding. Since he's early today, he takes the scenic route, riding through the city park, populated with young mothers and children playing on swing sets. Arriving at school, he puts his bike in the rack and locks it with a chain.

He enters the building, speaking to no one, walking down the hall with a blank yet pleasant look on his face. He goes into the cafeteria, which is bustling with activity prior to the start of classes. He walks up to a table full of jocks busy horsing around, which they do when they're not otherwise occupied with bullying people like R.T.

He stops several feet away, calling out, "Hey, assholes."

As they turn to see whom to beat up, he raises the handgun and fires. After dropping the four guys sitting at the table, he continues to fire, hitting two girls in the back as they try to escape. He then turns the gun on himself, pointing it at the side of his head, still looking pleasant and blank. He pulls the trigger.

47

ANOTHER
HIGH SCHOOL MEETING

Only days later, the school superintendent calls an urgent conference with the local prosecutor and the bereaved parents of the dead jocks. The meeting is taking place in the same cafeteria in which they met their recent demise. This is the same turf over which they will no longer reign in their terrorization of class nerds; however, no nerds are in attendance. Many of them are home, celebrating.

An angry father is squaring off with the prosecutor, one who's also getting sick of these meetings.

"What do you mean, you can't do anything? You're the goddamn prosecutor! Can't you arrest somebody?"

"Sir, I understand you're upset, but it's not that simple."

"What's not so simple? Some kid picks up his father's handgun, takes it to school, and blows away my boy! What can be simpler than that?"

"Well, I'd indict the shooter, but since he killed himself, there's no one else to charge."

"I don't understand. If his father put that gun in the kid's hand as he left for school and told him to shoot somebody, would you charge the father with a crime?"

"Yes. I believe we would charge him under such a circumstance with conspiracy or as an accessory."

"If he handed the gun to his kid but said nothing, could you still charge him?"

"Yes, I'm sure we'd still charge him with some form of criminal negligence if his kid didn't have a concealed-carry permit."

"So, what if the father leaves the gun lying around and his boy picks it up and kills my son? How is this different from a father handing the gun to his boy when he walks out the door? How does that change anything? You tell me! How is leaving a gun lying around different from putting it in a kid's hand?"

"Well, sir, it might seem the same to you, and I can understand your point, but the law has tied my hands. We have no rule mandating the securing of firearms from access by children or teenagers."

"This stuff will keep happening because no one ever holds an adult responsible. If the parents knew they were liable, maybe they'd think twice about leaving a loaded gun lying around the house to begin with."

"I suppose you're right, but like it or not, the firearm lobby is way too powerful to let us pass parental-liability laws for gun owners. Everybody wants his or her freedom. They just don't want responsibility."

"Freedom without responsibility is fine for an infant, not an adult. So if a kid runs over my son with his parents' car, we can sue the parents, but if he shoots my boy with his parents' gun, tough luck?"

"Yes. I guess that about sums things up. The firearm industry is more protected than General Motors."

The irate and distraught father is left speechless. He knows the prosecutor isn't responsible for making the laws. He could shout to the heavens. God might listen, but no one on Earth appears to be.

48

LARRY WINTERS

Ever the resourceful one, Maggie has secured an interview with Larry Winters, the former vice president of gun maker Holtz and Western, a company steeped in historical American lore. They kicked him out of corporate leadership back in 2000. As the firearm industry then had a friend in the White House in George W. Bush, Mr. Winters' services were no longer needed. He was what no gun manufacturer in the United States needs: a leader with a conscience.

Maggie pulls into the driveway of the Winters home in an area of older brick mansions. Larry, a graying man of around sixty-five years of age, greets her at the front door. After exchanging pleasantries, he escorts her to a comfortable sitting room.

"I'm pleased to meet you, Maggie. My wife and I have both been avid readers of your columns. I think you're a fair journalist, which is why I've allowed you to come into my home for this meeting. As a rule, I avoid being interviewed by members of the press. I don't trust them. All I require is for you to quote me accurately and faithfully."

Maggie takes a liking to this sincere and straightforward gentleman and wants to put him at ease. "Thank you for inviting me to your home, Mr. Winters."

"Larry."

"Larry it is and shall be. I wanted to ask you about the

situation surrounding your termination at Holtz and Western. Although I don't know all the details, the impression I get is that it was an acrimonious split."

"I'd say so. At some point, the board and myself had moved well beyond seeing things eye to eye."

"How so?"

"We in the firearm industry were coming under increasing pressure from the government to change how we did business. President Clinton reached out to us, trying to connect on a more constructive level rather than legislate bans on certain firearms."

"Did he contact you after the assault-weapons ban of 1994 was in place?"

"Yes, he did. There were massive loopholes in the law, and manufacturers concentrated on how to exploit those openings. The president even called me personally, appealing to my conscience, getting me onboard to work with him in trying to reduce gun violence. I felt he was making sense. What he and I agreed on shouldn't have ever turned into a partisan issue. I mean, what sort of human being should look the other way regarding public safety? Does everything need to be political? So I brought a few legitimate ideas to the company brass."

"How were they received by other members?"

"They didn't go over well at all, as you can understand. I hope you appreciate the irony that gun violence fuels our business."

"I can see where it would create an enormous conflict of interest. How were you able to reconcile the competing positions?"

"I tried to deal with things in as constructive a way as possible. To supplement a potential loss of revenue from no longer selling assault rifles to civilians, I attempted to steer the company into investing in other endeavors. I wanted to move into mountain biking and the outdoors, camping gear and attire. I believed our name could carry us into several areas, moving away from a core business concentrated strictly on supplying firearms."

"Did something happen that brought on a change in conscience?"

"There was no specific incident. This was more a process of gradual awareness, not of the product we were marketing, but how it was being marketed. What became obvious over time is that players in the industry focused only on sales volume, turning a blind eye toward where many of those guns would end up."

"Were you alone in your concerns? Did others in the company, or in other firearms companies you're aware of, ever express similar thoughts?"

"Well, I can tell you I wasn't the only one, at least among the board. Some would meet with me in private, encouraging me to take us in other directions. Elsewhere, the industry appeared to be less amenable to change."

"What did you and the president discuss?"

"We discussed if more could be done about assault weapons. He didn't do it to score political points. He knew it would cost him. I believe his only motivation was to do what was best for the country. Say what you will, but he cared about the welfare of the people he served."

"Did he have any specific suggestions?"

"No. He sought my advice on how to best keep military-grade firepower out of the wrong hands. More than that, we offered to reengineer our civilian weapons so as not to accept extended-ammunition magazines. We were also willing to establish a tighter rein on the whole supply chain, making a greater effort to shut down straw purchases of firearms by criminal fronts. I thought it would be good for the company name. We'd let the public know we were involved in their safety other than existing for no other reason than to dump as many guns on the street as possible."

"How did others in the business react?"

"It made us into a pariah. Rather than seeing it as an inspiration to expand their own horizons, they treated our moves with fear and hostility."

Maggie observes, "One might say fear and hostility are the bedrocks of your industry."

Larry grimaces at that statement. "I suppose you could see it that way. I guess a lack of either would be bad for business. Fear is our primary marketing tool."

"Did the other firearms companies turn on you?"

"No question. They were hostile. Their partners in the gun lobby responded by organizing a boycott against us. Unfortunately, it succeeded. Our revenue dropped by half almost overnight. The board threw me out. The result depressed the worth of Holtz and Western to where we ended up selling the company to one of these predators for ten cents on the dollar."

It stuns Maggie to hear how the gun lobby could bring down an American institution. "How have the people in this organization been able to wield such enormous, absolute power?"

"They can harness the resources of every other competitor. Their means are to divide and conquer. They're one of the most divisive organizations in the world today. Just like they rule the public through fear and intimidation, they ruled us. They will threaten anyone who dares step out of line, who moves once inch away from the official industry positions."

"What did you propose that made them the most upset?"

"It seems as if they were upset by our efforts to shut down straw purchases. We tried our best to close the pipeline to criminals. What really set them off was our efforts to develop a smart gun, which could only be fired by its owner. We were motivated by a concern for child safety."

"Why would that be a problem? You'd figure they would be just as concerned about arming the wrong person."

"You would think so. However, you also need to consider that without having more armed criminals roaming the streets, the public might be less scared into buying firearms. It may be hard to believe, but that's the dirty little secret in this industry. The more guns we supply to criminals, the more guns we can sell to law-abiding citizens. It's all about making a profit, whether that gun goes to a good neighbor or a bad criminal. As much as they like to claim otherwise, the gun lobby doesn't give one whit about the safety of you or your family. They don't care about the Second Amendment, and they don't care about self-defense. All they care about is selling as many guns as possible and bringing in as much revenue as possible."

49

PARK VALLEY HUNT CLUB

The Park Valley Hunt Club is holding its monthly gathering. Aside from the usual banter about the size of game bagged in the last month, other topics in the wide world of guns are bubbling to the surface. One of the club's charter members, Fred Thomas, asks to take the podium. The others have great respect for him. He is also head of the local VFW. The club president turns the floor over to him, so he begins.

"I'm a hunter. My dad was a hunter. His dad was a hunter. For many of us, this has been a family tradition. I'm proud of that and make no apologies to anyone, especially anyone who eats meat. There's nothing any more sacred about letting someone else slaughter your meal when you're buying it in the store rather than doing it with your own hands. I also wish to discuss a couple of matters today. I'll ask you all to please hear me out."

He continues. "Many here give money to the NRA, and some donate to other gun rights groups, too. I respect this, and I've done the same. Most of us are longtime members. However, I also believe we need to address certain tendencies that are becoming inherent in these organizations."

By the response, he has already said too much, as some in the audience become agitated at having their sensibilities questioned. One hunter offers a note of caution. "Be careful. You may step on a lot of toes."

Fred's character has been forged under fire, and he won't be silenced. "Look, I'm tired of how these organizations are taking our money and claiming to be supporting our hunting rights while focusing on different matters. Not only that, but they seem to politically align themselves with those who want to foul our streams and encroach on natural preserves. They're expanding gas and oil drilling on these lands, all in the name of more profit. I believe our own resources are being used to pay lobbyists for these big corporations."

This doesn't pass without comment from an audience member. "Well, what do you suggest we do? Should we include a note with our dues payment instructing them on how to spend our money?"

Fred has a ready response. "I figure we might be far more effective if we sent them an empty envelope. Now, that could get their attention."

The group laughs at the suggestion.

"I also wish to discuss another issue. Some of you will be upset, but I want to speak my piece anyway. I've got a problem with this new 'stand your ground' business.

The crowd appears uneasy.

"I believe this sets a bad precedent, and I don't think it keeps anyone safer. It makes this country a more dangerous place, not for criminals, but for honest, hard-working citizens, whether they be unarmed or armed to the teeth. Getting back to the original issue, this also has nothing to do with protecting our rights as hunters."

Some members feel the need to respond.

"I don't see a problem with the law."

"Yeah, works for me, too."

"Looks like you may be outnumbered here, Fred. You're not going soft on us, are you, buddy?"

"Come on, now. You guys know me better than that.

I've been in combat and taken a life, up close and personal. I'd do it again, too, if I had to. That's not the point. We don't want our neighborhoods and streets turned into a damn free-fire zone."

"They're looking that way now," chimes someone from the back of the room.

"No, they're not. You may think things are bad, but they can always turn worse. We shouldn't help speed up the process. This law's making it too easy to kill somebody and walk. You need to understand. This law doesn't create a safer environment for anyone in this room."

Others aren't so quick to agree. John Tally jumps to his feet. "Hey, I'm for anything that gives me the freedom to protect my family. I'm sure that goes for everyone here."

Fred is not about to accept the everyday talking points. "Oh, and how does it do that? How in the hell does this law make it easier to protect your family? Are you around them twenty-four hours a day? Where are your kids right now? Do you remember what it was like when you were a kid? Did any of you carry a gun when you were eighteen? I know I didn't. Eighteen-year-olds get into fights. Soon they'll be able to shoot one another at the least provocation and then walk away free with the 'I was scared' defense. 'Stand your ground,' my ass. I can see what's coming, and damned if I'm gonna let the country turn that way without a fight."

If he expects a fight, he need not look far. Again, John responds, "Oh, come on. I'm so sick of everybody blaming guns whenever some kid shoots somebody. We should find out who these troubled kids are before they shoot anyone."

Fred replies, "Well, I'm sick of people blaming everything on troubled kids, like this has nothing to do with guns. It has *everything* to do with guns! We've always had troubled kids, and we always will. They just weren't given the easy means to murder one another, not until we dumped three hundred million guns on the street. If you want to blame everything on troubled kids, then what about troubled adults? We talk about keeping guns out of the hands of troubled kids, but then insist every troubled adult should be able to carry one. Well, here's news for you. Troubled adults can be more dangerous than troubled kids! Shouldn't we bother to screen them out, too? Are we too damned lazy or too damned sissified to do anything? Hell, troubled cops aren't allowed to carry a gun. How come everyone else does?"

John possesses no shortage of gun-lobby talking points. "Hey, Fred. I hope you haven't forgotten about the Second Amendment?"

"No, I haven't forgotten about it, including the part that says, 'well regulated militia.' It doesn't say *un*regulated militia, but says *well* regulated. So using the Second Amendment as an argument against firearm regulation is phony as hell, just like the politicians that make it! As long as the victims belong to someone else's family and not their own, it's not their problem."

50

DAVE STOCKTON

Dave Stockton is winding up his nightly radio show. He has maintained his positions during the late-night shift for years. Every evening, it's the same thing: He's confronted by callers who can't understand why his opinions differ so much from those of his colleagues. Many of them listen to AM talk shows from dawn till dusk. What that means is they're getting bombarded with right-wing propaganda by Republican shills posing as radio hosts throughout their entire day. Rather than experience the outside world and form their own perspective, they are instead being spoon fed an alternative reality that bears little semblance or sense.

Why is it so easy to be dishonest with them? Dave knows the answer. Like many of us, they've grown up around people they can trust. They're accustomed to not being lied to. Their neighbors have been honest, their friends have been honest, and their families have been honest. This makes the most gullible of them ripe for the taking by those without scruples. These vultures, while attempting to cloak themselves in morality, waving the flag or whatever it is they do, will lie over and over without reprimand. They're pushing a specific worldview, as they're paid to do. Free from constraints, with the excuse it's all about showbiz and ratings, these mavens of the microphone do great damage to the collective psyche of this nation. Too many people take these clowns seriously.

Their unchecked power in a medium they've monopolized has grown to where they could convince half the population we were struck by Iraq on 9/11, evidence by damned. If you can fool the public we got attacked by the wrong country, either you're too smart or the public's too stupid. Regardless, bearing false witness is both immoral and a sin. That won't stop most hosts.

Dave devotes himself to speaking the truth in this phony environment. He has tried in vain to undo a tsunami-size wave of dishonesty day after day, and it has taken a toll. He wonders how he ever came to this hopeless fight and why he even bothers. Maybe some people can't sit by while they see others getting buried in bullshit.

What he has found most galling is the level of support shown to those who the sane among us would consider cold-blooded murderers. Many of the latest killers making the news have received an unbelievable amount of help from the public, in both the emotional and financial sense. Although they criticized him for it, Barack Obama was right to size these people up as "clinging to their guns and their religion," in that exact order of importance. For them, the expression "Those who live by the sword, die by the sword" is just some biblical fantasy. They should try cracking the Bible once in a while.

Dave has a sympathetic ear in his engineer, Juan. Dave can count on him to lighten the mood when things become too much. This is most of the time. What doesn't help is that he isn't following his own self-imposed rule of not listening to other talk shows. He has found they're easy to avoid during the day, yet he tunes in on the way to his shift at the station. He hasn't been chilling out to some classical or jazz music while driving. Rather, he uses the opportunity to gird up on whatever nonsense he'll be forced to counter once he gets behind the microphone. This nonsense comes in nightly reruns of *The Ted Hunter Show*. Sometimes, it makes Dave want to hit himself in the head with a hammer. Other times, he feels the healthier impulse of wanting to nail Ted.

On this evening, Dave has been listening to Ted roll out the red carpet for Bob Cooper. The denizens of gun world, Ted's prime audience, are treating him like some kind of American hero. One caller after another claims Bob had every right to murder that Rogers kid. Many of them seem envious that he got to shoot a minority and get away with it. A good chunk of them fantasize about doing just that. This also thrills firearms dealers to no end. They've become wealthy off sick fantasies.

As far as his decision to pop up on Ted's show, it would appear Bob either ignored the advice of his attorney or doesn't even have one. However, Bob's lawyer needn't worry, as Ted lobs a series of softball questions. This guy ain't Nancy Grace, let alone Nancy Drew.

"So, Bob, as I understand it, you were walking down the sidewalk, keeping to yourself, when this Rogers monster jumped out of the bushes and attacked you. Is that how it happened?"

The outrageous liberties Ted takes with the facts also stuns Bob. He must not listen to the show too often.

"Um, yeah, that pretty much sums it up. I was just minding my own business."

"Bob, you are a true hero. This country needs more patriots like you, unafraid to exercise your Second Amendment right. I hope you put this perp down hard."

Now taking on the sternest of tones, Ted lectures his audience. As usual, he lays it on thick.

"This is a lesson for you all. You never know when you're gonna get jumped by some guy like this Rogers kid.

You need to be prepared and to protect yourself. I'm telling you, folks, we should throw these liberals out of office. They want to take our guns away, making all of us helpless. This Socialist Obama wants everyone unarmed and therefore unable to shoot agents from the IRS when they come to our homes demanding unpaid taxes. Firearms are our last line of defense against an oppressive government."

Turning back to his guest, "Bob, have they allowed you to keep your guns while this situation, this annoyance you have to go through, goes to trial?"

"Um, no. They confiscated all three of my handguns as a condition of my probation."

Ted keeps whipping it up. "How about that? Here you are, defending yourself against some dangerous maniac, doing the only reasonable thing you can do by putting him down. So, what does this government do? They take away the means for you to defend yourself. What are you expected to do next time one of these maggots jumps out of the bushes, use harsh language? Isn't this supposed to be a free country?"

Bob's attorney, if he hasn't already walked off the job, needn't worry. As usual, Ted has been doing most of the talking, thus denying his client the opportunity to hang himself. The upside is that this national media exposure has also given his client the chance to promote a website devoted strictly to his defense. Hell, the public might as well wire the money straight into the lawyer's bank account, as that's where the bulk of it will end up.

Dave shows up for work after sitting through this torturous excuse of an interview. As usual, he arrives at the station in a bad mood, no doubt induced by this aural onslaught. He doesn't have the good sense to change the channel or, better still, enjoy the silence. Then again, knowing what's coming makes for essential preparation. One caller after another wants to talk about Bob, most of them taking his side. They also attack the few sensible callers. This goes on throughout the show.

Dave reaches the completion of his air shift, mostly intact. He's not at the end of his rope, just close. At least the show tonight didn't approach to level of lunacy he encountered after the mass theater shooting in Aurora, Colorado. This occurred on a Friday night, during the premiere of the new Batman film. As expected, the right wing was out in force only seconds later, blaming it on the movie. They should blame it on the popcorn, too, if not the Goobers. In fact, it was a goober with an assault rifle that caused the damage.

Dave, like the rest of the United States, has gotten an earful throughout the weekend and is primed for his Monday night air shift. He's broken his vow to avoid talk radio, listening all day long. It has been a constant stream of phone calls, whipped up in part by the other hosts on the station. They're directing their ire at those liberals and their dreaded gun-free zones.

Gun-free zones, as the 'guns are the answer' crowd refers to them, get blamed for most of the recent mass shootings. This isn't established by facts, but by repetition of gun-lobby talking points. When the resident right-wing contributor to the local newspaper claimed this in an editorial, Dave had to respond. He fired off a letter to the editor, which to his surprise, got published. He pointed out some convenient examples where gun-free zones proved effective when enforced: major-league sporting events, along with concerts, etc. One can only imagine if the crowds could carry their guns to an NFL game. No player from either team would be safe, and that goes triple for the referees. You wouldn't want to attend a game wearing the opposing team's jersey, either. In fact, you wouldn't want to attend the game at all, since nobody would dare walk out on the field. There'd be no game.

On his way to the station the next night, Dave once again can't resist listening to *The Ted Hunter show*. Ted's guest is, of all people, that rock-and-roll monstrosity and UGO board member in good standing, Jim Savage. Although Jim ducked the military draft, he's still in favor of shooting anything that moves. It's his means of celebrating our cultural heritage. On this evening and most others, he brings on the heritage while leaving the culture at home.

"The entire problem, Ted, is the little sign at the entrance to the movie theater barring the patrons from exercising their God-given right to self-defense. Yes, you can blame it on the image of that gun in a circle with a line through it. Imagine if the moviegoers could shoot back in defending themselves."

A caller having the temerity to question Jim's astute observations has slipped past the screener. Ted introduces him as "Will from Milwaukee." Jim, also being from Wisconsin, gives him a warm greeting.

"So, Mr. Savage..."

"Call me Jim."

"So, Jim, although you may have avoided going to Vietnam, I didn't. I was a gunnery sergeant."

Ted jumps in with his typical brown nosing. "We salute you for your service to this country."

He attempts to further talk over Will before dismissing him altogether, but Will is persistent.

"Mr. Savage, you've obviously never been in a real firefight. It's not so cut and dry. Even in broad daylight, let alone the confines of a darkened theater, having multiple shooters firing at once results in lots of things being hit by stray bullets. Add to this the fact that in a movie theater, no one is wearing a uniform. So, Jim, you tell me, how is anyone supposed to know who to shoot at when they're surrounded by others who are also firing away? If one of the innocent moviegoers should shoot another innocent moviegoer during this free-for-all, is he now guilty of murder? How do you tell the good guys from the bad guys?"

Jim tries to stammer a response, but Will isn't finished with him. "Another thing, Jim: How come when I go to see you in concert, I can't bring a firearm? I mean, I know I won't run into any people of color inside one your shows, but how about outside the hall? Sorry, I couldn't resist throwing that in. Why do you insist that everyone should carry a gun everywhere else except to your concerts?"

Ted can't handle this logic, and cuts off him off. In the time-honored tradition of talk radio, he knows he can dispatch a caller while then berating him once there's no longer the chance of a response.

"Sorry, Jim. Some liberal thought he could disrupt the show. I'm sure he lied to the call screener just to get on the air with that insane rant. I should have cut him off a long time ago."

They continue to obsess over Second Amendment rights, while denigrating all liberals for having the audacity to attempt an exercise of their First Amendment rights.

For a rare moment, Dave shows up for his shift in an upbeat mood. He enjoyed hearing the smug world of Ted and Jim get pierced by someone who exhibits a modicum of sense.

As weeks pass by, even the most horrific of events recede into memory. This is the case in a society that appears to be moving with ever more speed. It seems to work to the advantage of the gun lobby that the time between mass shootings continues to shrink. Each fresh shooting pushes the last one into the distant past. "We should do something" has turned into a repetitive and meaningless battle cry, drowned out by the "more guns equals less crime" crowd. If 300 million guns aren't enough to make us safe, 310 million ought to do it, for sure. You hear this cockamamie rhetoric daily in the world of talk radio.

Dave can always count on Juan to provide comic relief. As he feels like a lone voice in the wilderness, Juan has become his Tonto. When in combat, you've got to have a wingman.

As the months pass by, a presidential election takes place. In radio land, full-time vilification of any Democratic incumbent is a given, and that goes double for one who's half-black. The amount of venom directed at Barack Obama from the far right is relentless. Every caller appears obsessed with some aspect of Obama's personal life and how it should be an absolute disqualifier.

"He wasn't even born here! Where's his birth certificate?"

This is one of Dave's favorite types of callers. He answers questions such as this with a request for them to send in a copy of *theirs*. None have taken him up on it yet. Perhaps they don't want to get on some register. Dave tries to reassure them that the station doesn't compile a list of dummies.

During the pre-election run-up, voter registration has become a big issue. The Republican Party is doing everything in their power to keep raising the bar, lest the contest be compromised by nonexistent voter fraud. In the land of talk radio, most callers sympathize with these efforts. It's at least nice to know they can feel some kind of sympathy about *something*.

"What's the matter with these people? All they ever do is whine. Why is it a big deal for an eighty-five-year-old black woman who's voted for sixty years to produce a birth certificate? Why can't she show three additional forms of identification?"

"So what if they don't have a driver's license?"

"What's wrong if they have to miss work catching a bus to the board of elections?"

"So what if there's a six-hour wait?"

"So what if the Republican Secretary of State has undermanned all the urban voting precincts?"

Dave attempts to address these questions, trying without success to get the callers to quit choking on their own bile. It's a wasted effort, as talk radio has long become a repository for the constant exchange of just such bile. He knows attempting to impart basic psychology to the audience gets lost on most. These days, this medium exists as an outlet for those consumed with hatred. It gives them a target as to whom or what to project that hatred onto.

The commercial breaks provide Dave with a mini oasis. They also give Juan an opportunity to make his usual fantasy suggestions.

"Maybe we could rig up some kind of hate meter, something that measures voice stress. I'll bet some of our callers could send that thing off the charts."

Dave chuckles at the thought. "You might have to stand back. A device like that could explode."

"You know, we could turn it into a nightly contest to see which caller drives the meter highest."

He considers the possibilities. "That's a good idea. We'll have engineering jump right on it. Or we could send an official request up to corporate and they can get back to us in six months."

They continue to banter about the logistics. At least it makes more sense than most of the callers. They also agree that a lie detector should become an essential part of any on-air gizmo. Juan comes up with a great suggestion.

"I know such devices exist, and I'm sure most of the

listeners will believe it, too. Since this is radio, we're unable to show an actual contraption. Having people *think* we have one would be sufficient."

They both begin to crack up, just imagining the possibilities. The more they think about it, the more they like the simplicity. Besides, they've both been at this long enough to spot a fat lie faster than any electronic tool in existence.

"Let's rig up a buzzer. We'll each have our own button, and whoever picks up the lie first can trigger it."

Juan has a bank of audio effects he triggers by the press of a button, a fixture at most stations.

"We'll load recordings of buzzers into the sound bank using different sounds. The bigger the fabrication, the more outrageous the buzz."

Dave is enjoying this. Radio stopped being fun for him long ago. Doing this has restored a lost sense of adventure. "The biggest whoppers of all will set off a siren!"

The following night, he shows up at the station looking forward to doing his air shift for a change. He has been too preoccupied with new ideas to bother listening to Ted Hunter on the way to work, thus sparing himself the torture.

The first buzzer goes off less than five minutes into the show. Someone with an obsession about gun rights describes for listeners the two different occasions where he has saved someone's life by pulling out a handgun. It's easy to smoke these guys out. They are familiar with Dave's position on the deadly combination of guns, idiots, and concealed-carry licenses. As a result, some new caller may attempt to regal the audience with recollections of his astounding feats of bravery, gun in hand. The reason it's always a new caller is because the regular ones know better.

One of the first tip-offs is that these heroic deeds so often come in pairs. Eager to make a point, many of them embellish their achievements by multiplying their occurrences. As Dave has sat through more of these ramblings than he can count, he can't resist piercing their story under cross-examination. These stories tend to whither under the cross.

Over the ensuing weeks, the lie-detecting buzzer has become perhaps too effective, as the callers are now becoming conditioned to being on their best behavior. This means no more whoppers. In fact, eventually Dave announces to the audience he's suspending the practice. It's not a matter of choice, as he figures if he continues down this path much longer, no one will call anymore.

51

THE MEETING

The door to William Kohler's office bursts open. He puts his phone call on hold, greeting his star investigative reporter. He can see the look of excitement and urgency on her face. He turns his attention to the caller.

"Yes…that's great. Something's come up. I need to get back. Thanks."

He turns to Maggie. "I haven't seen you so stoked in a long time."

"There's a good reason for it, Bill. We may haul in a big fish."

"Well, you've sure baited *me*. Who are we talking about?"

"William Underwood."

"Senator William Underwood?"

"The one and only."

"He's head of the Senate Committee on Appropriations. That makes him the most powerful and influential member of the US Congress. What have you got on him?"

Now she has his full, undivided attention. "Well, I have nothing on him yet, but I see an opportunity coming up to nail him but good. A source in his office tells me he has an upcoming meeting at the downtown Hilton. John Rumsen, head of the Armstrong Firearms Company, has set it up. They will join Cal Trachert, chief lobbyist for UCON. Everything is top secret."

The news intrigues Bill. "So they're getting together for drinks. What else have we got?"

"We are expecting money to change hands, a sizeable amount."

"How do you know this?"

"My source, who functions as his secretary, has been eavesdropping on the senator's phone calls. Ever since he first tried to put his hand up her skirt, she's had it in for him. She tells me she can still feel the cold metal of his wedding ring brushing up against her thigh."

Now Bill is skeptical. "So we've got possible influence peddling. That and a nickel will get you a cup of coffee, $2.50 at Starbucks."

Maggie is unfazed by his reaction. "Make that one million in cash, the first installment of a five-million-dollar payoff."

"The whole thing looks suspicious, but I'm sure he'll just weasel out of any accusations by filing this as a campaign contribution."

"Cash? We're talking millions in cash! You know damn well it won't get filed under anything. This is a flat-out bribe, and I'll bet my salary it will be unreported income. This should land him nowhere but in a federal penitentiary."

He still appears skeptical. "What's the quid pro quo? I'm sure the senator isn't getting paid for his good looks."

"It's all about federalizing firearm restrictions. They're paying him off to introduce and push a bill to nationalize all gun laws. The goal is to allow unrestricted concealed-carry privileges and blanket immunity for all Americans with firearms who claim a 'stand your ground' defense whenever they commit a shooting."

"Let's not get too carried away. How did you come to

possess such level of detail? How ironclad is this information?"

"My source has never let me down. I've known her for many years."

"So she claims to have overheard a phone call or what?"

"She overheard nothing. The senator told her."

"Why would he be so stupid?"

"Because he's infatuated with her, that's why. He's cheating on his wife and wants to run away with a member of his staff, one he's so smitten by he'll tell her anything. Besides, the Swiss bank account he's wiring the funds to is in her name."

"That would make her a coconspirator. She could end up in prison, too."

"She wouldn't if the money doesn't get wired, instead getting turned over to federal prosecutors as evidence."

"She's not tempted by such a sum?"

"No. She can't stand the old coot. I think she cares more about his wife. She'd love to stick it to him on the way out the door."

"Washington would be through with her."

"It doesn't matter. She's through with Washington."

William thinks it over. "If the money's coming from UCON, then it must come from the Kovach brothers."

This causes Maggie's eyes to go wide. These two billionaires are the driving force behind UCON. "We could land the biggest fish in the Senate, and a couple of whales, too. It's illegal to bribe a United States senator."

"These guys aren't stupid enough to get their hands dirty. They would keep themselves far removed from such activity."

"Yes, I've considered that. Sometimes it doesn't hurt

to overturn a few rocks. When the spotlight shines on them, some people overreact, implicating others."

"Don't hold your breath. Fear of prosecution doesn't affect those who can afford to buy the judge."

"Well, at least we could nail a corrupt senator."

William muses, "Who? I have an even bigger challenge for you. Try to find an honest one."

They share a laugh, although the joke's way too obvious. He again becomes serious. "Hearsay isn't good enough. It'll require something more substantial, ironclad evidence, leaving nothing to interpretation or chance. What we need is an actual recording of these conversations."

"We can do better than that, Bill. How would you like a videotape of the money changing hands?"

"Now that would do it. Once the broadcast networks get hold of an incriminating video, all bets are off."

Ever cautious, William wants to know the logistics of the operation. He has never been a big fan of espionage in the name of journalism. That's a knife that can cut both ways. "How would we set this up? Where will the meeting take place?"

"My sister-in-law is the assistant manager of the downtown Hilton. Senator Underwood stays there when in town. He likes to use that hotel for his numerous trysts. He always books a room under the name Perrywinkle. They've reserved a suite in that name for next Tuesday. My source in the senator's office has confirmed he's set a meeting for that date."

The two sit in contemplation, thinking about the implications. William breaks the silence.

"The Feds need authorization from a judge. Considering who's involved, that'll be hard to get. In fact, they could quash the whole plan. The more I think about it, the worse our chances look."

He isn't about to dissuade Maggie. "How about if we videotape this ourselves?"

"It would be illegal."

"There must be something we can do. We can't pass up an opportunity like this." She mulls over possible courses of action. "What if a third party videotaped the encounter, then handed us the tapes? We'll claim they're from a protected source. We'd just be reporting the news."

William brightens again. "I suppose it wouldn't be illegal for us to inform someone about a meeting taking place if we weren't to enter any compensatory agreement. We would not be responsible if this third party transcribed a visual and audible documentation of the event on his or her own accord. Devoid of any payment, it's not against the law to accept these videotapes if the third party were to hand them over. Do you have anyone in mind?"

Maggie has a ready reply. "I have a PI that I've used before. This guy is reliable and very discreet. I trust him, and he trusts me. He'll serve as our unnamed source. As far as compensation goes, let's say we'll get caught up down the road. Besides, I'm sure he'd love to clock this senator for sport. He's not a big fan of the US Congress."

"Yeah, him and ninety percent of the country."

52

THE STEELE TRIAL

The trial of the State of Florida versus Randy Steele is underway. Randy is on the witness stand. Lewis Darby would tend to keep his client from testifying under most circumstances. However, he has decided the best course of action, in this case, will be to present him to the world. He now stands before the defendant, leading him through testimony.

"Mr. Steele, you are a veteran of the Iraq war, isn't that correct?"

"Yes, sir. I served two tours."

"You've also received the bronze star for bravery in combat, is that not correct?

"Yes, it is."

"This makes you an American hero."

The prosecutor jumps up. "Objection!"

Judge Joseph T. Corcoran concurs. He finds lawyers will say anything to sway a jury. "Sustained. The jury will ignore those remarks."

Lewis continues. "As a veteran of combat, they trained you to act instinctively when you see someone drawing a weapon. Is that not so?"

"Yes."

"Acting reflexively can make all the difference between life and death, yes?"

"Yes."

"So when the officer drew his weapon, you responded in a way they trained you to do, correct?

At this, the prosecutor jumps up again. "Objection! The officer did not draw his firearm. We have it right on the dash cam."

Lewis stands his ground. "The officer was reaching for his gun. We've all seen this on the video."

The judge says, "I'll allow the question."

The prosecutor won't let that stand. "Your Honor, the officer is trained to put his hand near the holster as a precaution. We can't divine intent beyond that."

"I said I'd allow the question."

The prosecutor sits down, exasperated.

Lewis proceeds. "Mr. Steele, you saw the officer touch the handle of his gun, didn't you?"

The prosecutor says, "Objection! We haven't been able to determine that from the video."

The judge replies, "I'll allow it." Turning to the defendant, the judge directs him to answer.

"Hell, yes. He was going for his gun."

Lewis asks, "You're also aware we've had an epidemic of police brutality in this town, aren't you?"

The prosecutor cries again, "Objection!"

"Sustained. The jury will strike the last remark. Rephrase the question, Mr. Darby."

"Mr. Steele, you're aware that sometimes the police shoot innocent people, are you not?"

The prosecutor goes ballistic. "Objection!"

"Sustained. The jury will ignore those remarks. Mr. Darby, you're skating on thin ice."

"Sorry, Your Honor. Let me rephrase the question. Mr. Steele, as you were being pulled over, didn't you recall an incident on the TV show *Law and Order* where a cop shot an innocent man?"

"Objection!"

"I'll allow it." The judge knows Lewis is clever.

The prosecutor again jumps out of his chair. "Your Honor! This is insane!"

Now it's the prosecutor that's skating on thin ice. If there's one thing Judge Corcoran doesn't care for, it is having the sanity of either himself or his court called into question. "Another outburst and I'll hold you in contempt!"

Lewis is enjoying this. "Mr. Steele, when this man reached for his weapon, didn't you have every reason to fear for your life?"

"Yes."

"To you, this was a dangerous man with a gun, an immediate threat to your life, correct?"

"Objection! He's leading the witness!"

"I'll allow it."

"But..."

"I'll allow it. Continue."

"Did you feel, when the man reached for his gun, your life was about to end?"

"Yes."

"And you allowed your instincts, those they taught you in the service of this great nation, to take over?"

"Yes sir, I did."

53

NEWS OF THE DAY

A reporter stands outside the courthouse, broadcasting live to the nation.

"It was another explosive day in the trial of the State of Florida versus Randy Steele. The Iraq war veteran is charged in the murder of Officer Charles Morrison during a routine traffic stop. Final arguments will be made tomorrow. Back to you, Mark."

Mark Corker continues from the studio.

"In other local news today, Parnell Hinton has pleaded not guilty to shooting a McDonald's employee at the drive-through window after complaining about the long wait. Elsewhere, a family of four is dead tonight after a man walked into a Chuck E. Cheese and opened fire on his estranged wife. Also killed were his nine-year-old son and five-year-old daughter. Both were there to celebrate the daughter's birthday."

His mood then brightens as he turns to matters of greater interest to the average American, such as the weather. "Now let's hear from everyone's favorite weather lady, Sandy Roundtree. Tell us, Sandy, are we in for more sunny days this week?"

"We sure are, Mark."

Like most weather ladies, Sandy is bubbling, regardless of her news lead-in. "We're expecting a hot weekend. Remember to grab the SPF 35 before you head to the beach."

54

CLOSING ARGUMENTS

Closing arguments in the Steele trial have begun. The prosecutor is speaking to the jury.

"Ladies and gentlemen, this case couldn't be more simple. The defendant is charged with killing an officer of the law in cold blood. You've all seen this on the dash-cam video, and it can't be any more obvious. I'm asking you to find this man guilty. To do otherwise would set a dangerous precedent. One thing in this land that is sacrosanct is our respect for the law. Without it, our society would fall apart. Yet the defense asks you to suspend this belief and excuse him for this inexcusable act. You should not. We cannot allow the murder of a policeman while in the lawful, rightful discharge of his duty. You would send a message out to every thug, every criminal, that it's OK to shoot a cop, as easy as calling it self-defense. Is this the country we want for ourselves, for our families? The law is sacred, and this case cries out for justice. I know you'll do what's right."

He winds up his remarks on that note.

The judge addresses the packed courtroom. "The court will take a thirty-minute recess, after which the defense arguments will begin." He hits the gavel.

The half hour flies by for all except Randy, for whom it seems like an eternity. The closing argument resumes as Lewis makes statements to the jury on behalf of the defendant.

"Ladies and gentlemen of the jury, this may be one of the most important cases of our lifetime. I need to ask you to look at the big picture. The actions of Mr. Steele aren't the only thing on trial. No, we're looking at something much more important. What's at stake is the freedom of every American citizen to defend himself or herself at all times and under all circumstances to stand his or her ground. Each of us has loved ones, people we care about. I know each of us believe we and our loved ones have the right to defend ourselves, whether our attacker is in plain clothes or wearing a badge."

Lewis pauses for emphasis, looking each individual member of the jury in the eye as he speaks. "Just imagine yourself in Mr. Steele's position. Here he is, a decorated combat veteran who served this country with distinction, a soldier who put his life on the line for every single one of you. Our government trained this man to defend himself and to defend us all against those who would do us harm. In this situation, my client, an innocent citizen minding his own business, was defending himself from what he perceived to be an armed assailant. The defendant in this trial is more than Mr. Steele. The future of the 'stand your ground' law is what's at stake. This law is protecting the lives of you, your children, and anybody you care about. If you find my client guilty, you'll be deciding that none of us have the right to protect ourselves. Your decision will determine the fate of this law. If you find my client guilty, this law may be overturned, and you would thus force yourselves and your families to be helpless against attack."

Lewis is aware he's laying it on thick, but also knows timidity won't win this case.

"Can any of you say, without a reasonable doubt, Randy Steele would be alive today if he hadn't exercised his right to defend himself, to stand his ground? No, of course you couldn't. The future of this country and its law-abiding citizens is in your hands. Therefore, you must, for God's sake, you *must* find my client, Mr. Steele, not guilty. Thank you, and may God bless this great nation, and each and every one of you."

These over-the-top closing remarks leave the prosecutor speechless. Remarkably, he waives the opportunity to make any further rebuttal, assuming no jury in all creation would be stupid enough to fall for this steaming pile. One thing he chose to overlook is old the adage "You can never underestimate the intelligence of the American people." This line was written long before the rise and influence of modern-day talk radio, *Right-Wing News*, and the Internet. Prior to these times, in comparison, the public was positively brilliant.

55

JIM'S TOUR PREPARATIONS

Having allowed himself to get baited into agreeing to book his upcoming spring tour only at venues that will allow the audience to carry firearms, Jim Savage's latest outing has officially been billed as the Play 'Em and Slay 'Em Tour. The crew has dubbed it the Duck and Cover Tour behind Jim's back. The members of his band are furious with him for having agreed to this stunt. They vote to wear "I'm Not Jim" T-shirts, lest a far-off marksman hit the wrong target.

Rehearsals have become chaotic affairs. Besides learning the right chords, the musicians are being forced to focus on the concertgoers and not on their guitar necks. This may cause some flubbed notes and missed key changes, but you never know when they might need to duck fast behind the PA system. At one point, Jim and his manager consider positioning snipers up on top of the speaker columns. However, the snipers nixed that idea, refusing to be sitting ducks.

As much as they all wish the attention would die down, it has instead taken on a life of its own. Cable news is all abuzz with this story. The great Jim Savage will attempt to do what no other concert act or professional sports team has done in the modern age: perform for a pistol-packing audience. Ticket sales are unusually robust, considering Jim hasn't drawn a sizeable crowd in years. It soon dawns on him

and his management that all these tickets being sold are going to both friend and foe alike. This could turn into a NA-
SCAR-type event where some of the more morbid fans only
attend hoping to witness a big crash. He concedes to spring-
ing for Kevlar outfits for himself and the rest of the band.
In hopes they'll be spared, the roadies vote to wear police
uniforms. Even the T-shirt vendors have lowered their usual stratospheric prices. They don't want to stand accused of
armed robbery by armed customers.

Although his last visit to a radio station burned him,
his manager goads Jim into accepting another interview. This
time, it's conducted by a caustic morning-show jock, Matty
Waters.

"Here he is folks, the one and only, the Milwaukee ma-
rauder, Jim Savage!"

Matty's engineer patches in a sound effect of massive
applause.

"Hey there, man. How are preparations for your upcoming tour coming along?"

"Oh, they're going super."

"That's good to know."

Jim is here to talk about the music, which, as he should
have expected, interests neither the host nor the audience.
"Yeah, Matt, we've got a dynamite set planned for our fans.
We'll be playing all the hits."

"Speaking of hits, Jim, are you expecting a hit to be
made on you? As most of us are aware, you're encouraging
everyone to carry concealed weapons to the shows."

Jim tries to walk it back. "Well, I wouldn't say we're
encouraging it. Let's just say we will allow it."

"I'm not picking up a tinge of regret, am I? After all,
this is what you're all about. It's what you stand for, right?
Hell, we're looking forward to the show. I'm bringing my Ru-

ger, and my wife is bringing her Glock. If someone at the concert gets out of line, we could get in some target practice."

"It won't be necessary. My fans all love me. There shouldn't be any problem."

"Don't forget, Mark David Chapman loved John Lennon, too," Matt points out. "Don't worry, we've got your back, man."

Jim's coming to regret this whole fiasco-in-the-making by the minute. Matt's pumped up. "Let's go to the phone lines. Rob from Bedford, you're on the air."

"Hey, Matt. Hey, Jim."

"So, Rob, tell Jim what type of firearm you plan on bringing to the concert."

"I'm bringing my AR-15. I've got a special harness that will allow me to wear it under my coat so it'll be concealed. It might be my last chance to blast somebody before that commie Obama outlaws these things."

Jim sits in stone silence, unable to respond, contemplating what he and his mouth have wrought. Matt remains engaged in the conversation. "What kind of gun will your date be carrying to the concert?"

"Um, I don't have a date."

"When's the last time you've had one?"

"Ah, it's been quite a while. What the heck? I don't need one anyway. I've got my guns, and I've got the Internet. You can meet lots of hot chicks online. You should see some of these pictures!"

"Oh, I'll bet they're hot, Rob. Is there something you'd like to ask Jim?"

"Um, yeah, hi there, Jim."

"How are you, Rob?"

"Oh, just great, thanks. I'm really looking forward to the show. It should be great, being surrounded by like-minded individuals, if you get what I mean. Hey, Jim, I just wanted to ask you, what kind of gun do you pack when you're performing onstage?"

"Well, I ah, I don't carry a gun with me onstage. It would get in the way."

"What about when you get off the stage? I mean, you can't always count on security, can you? Celebrities like you need to be ready at all times. You never know. You know?"

"Yeah, I guess so."

"Don't worry, Jim. We'll all be packing, so we'll look out for you. What could go wrong?"

Jim's head is busy spinning with all kinds of things that could go wrong. This won't be his most relaxed tour.

"Jeff from Toledo, you're on the air with Jim Savage."

"Hey there, Matt and Jim. How's it going?"

"Terrific, thanks." At least it is for Matt.

"So Jim, I've been looking forward to seeing you for a long time, but my girlfriend is refusing to come. This whole gun thing makes her kind of upset. I guess one of her cousins got shot last week."

"Hey, it happens. Our prayers go out to her and her cousin, and here's to a speedy recovery."

"Um, he's dead."

"Well, our prayers go out to her."

The angry girlfriend grabs the phone out of Jeff from Toledo's hand. "Hello, Jim. This is Molly. Look, I don't need your prayers. I'll tell you what would make a much bigger difference than your lame offer of prayer. This clown that shot my cousin couldn't legally buy a gun, thanks to his long rap sheet. So he bought one instead from a local gun show. It was one of those gun shows you and your butt buddies at UGO fought to keep open. My cousin would still be alive today if not for you, you stupid jerk. So you can take your guns, along

195

with your obviously little dick, and shove 'em where the..."

Matt hits the dump button, cutting off the call.

"Sorry, folks. We've got a lot of cranks out there. I hope that skank gets the same thing that happened to her cousin. She and her boyfriend should stay home. Besides, I have it on good authority that Jim has a generous endowment."

Jim winces at the direction this conversation has taken. Although he'd love to end the interview, Matt takes another call.

"Hi, this is Chuck."

"Where are you from, Chuck?"

"Never mind where I'm from. Maybe it's you that needs to worry about where you're from."

"What's that supposed to mean?"

"Did you ever see the movie *Talk Radio*?"

This movie portrays every talk-show host's worst nightmare: ending up on the receiving end of a fruitcake with a gun. Matt lies. "Never caught it. Don't care to. Goodbye, Chuck."

Now rattled, he hits the wrong button, thus unable to cut off the call.

"I want to say something to Jim. I'll be there at your concert, buddy. I've bought my ticket, and when I get there, I'm going to punch *your* ticket, too. I've got a permit to carry, and I'll be packing. No one's going to stop me. Don't plan on booking any more shows because this one's going to be your last. You'll never even see it coming. I'm gonna give you something real to suck on."

After pounding the cutoff button to where it's become nonfunctional, Matt's engineer comes to the rescue, cutting off the threatening call. Matt is rattled.

"Sorry, Jim. I don't know how that guy got past our screener. Can we trace that?"

The engineer shakes his head, mouthing, "No."

"Or not. Well, I guess this world's full of dangerous people. We all need to carry guns, in case we run into a guy like that."

Now Jim tries to reassure the host. "Don't worry, Matt. Guys who make threats seldom carry them out."

Although this is true, Jim also knows the guys he needs to watch out for don't announce their intentions on talk shows. They're the ones that cause him to lose sleep. If he makes it to the end of this tour, it will be a miracle. Just getting through this radio show might take one.

56

DAVE'S LAST BROADCAST

In the audacious world of talk radio, one can't help but go numb from exposure to the slanted, daily barrage of biased opinion disguised as news. How the many conditioned callers react to events can further depress one's spirit. Some bring perceptive views and insights about human nature. Then again, there are the others.

For Dave Stockton, it has all come to a head after the tragic elementary school shooting in Newtown, Connecticut. People in the nation were shaken from their slumber by this grotesque display of lethal firepower used on the least defensible among us. This event has also encouraged the firearm industry apologists to slither out from under their collective rock. They have taken this opportunity to once again sneer at the rest of society, not caring one whit about twenty dead children. Incredibly, the shock of that catastrophe has been trumped in gun world by the selfishness of many of its most vociferous members. They're more preoccupied with their own personal access to these murderous adult toys than they are with concerns for present, past, and future victims. The cries of children have been drowned out by the whining of immature, gun-worshiping adults for whom no magazine has a high enough capacity.

After suffering through many years of trying to correct the record, the time has come for Dave to hang it up.

Rather than go quietly into the night, he leaves his radio audience with a heart-felt epilogue.

"One thing I've always had difficulty with is to stay silent while confronted by people engaged in the dissemination of a lie. Any lie can qualify, small or large. Something about it makes my skin crawl, prompting me to speak out. Thus, my choice of profession for the past number of years is rather curious.

"Hosting a talk radio show, at least since the industry deregulation of 1996, has offered one of two options: either going along or being honest. I made my choice long ago. Perhaps my parents could have raised me with fewer scruples, as it may have made this profession more profitable.

"For millions of regular, albeit exclusive listeners of talk radio, it can be the only contact they have with the outside world. It is the medium through which they receive their worldview. This puts an enormous responsibility on the shoulders of the national networks of talk-show hosts. Unfortunately, the moral sense of obligation toward the audience to regard their collective intelligence with respect is lacking. Instead, they treat people like saps.

"The bottom line in the radio business, not unlike most businesses, is of primary importance. A proven approach to bringing home the big numbers is to rely on the oldest rhetorical trick in the book—keeping the audience outraged. This keeps a certain percentage of the population riveted and tuned in. The more people stay tuned in, the more stations and networks can charge for advertising, and the more they reward their hosts. Truthfulness has become an unnecessary and perhaps counterproductive aspect of the equation.

"The easiest way to keep an audience mad is to give them something to be mad *at*. Some of the more obvious, everyday examples of convenient targets are Hillary Clinton or

Barack Obama. Any liberal will do. It's the classic posturing of 'us versus them' that works so well in radio world. This is a necessary component of any con. You're conditioned to trust a lying spokesperson, not your lying eyes.

"If you spend the day listening to a constant stream of talk radio, you're just spending your time soaking up the Republican National Committee talking points. They're furnished daily to the networks. This results from the aforementioned industry deregulation, part of the Telecommunications Act of 1996. The fine print in the act enabled a handful of party operatives waiting in the wings to scoop up the vast majority of stations, thus monopolizing the message. The people are trusting to where they assume that repetition of certain stock lines by myriad hosts is nothing more than a coincidence.

"However, I don't want to just sit here and complain. I would like to offer something more constructive to those who find it disconcerting to face the mindless, agenda-driven nonsense. This applies whether you're at a local coffee shop, watering hole, or the family dinner table. Ask folks if they've heard an identical statement uttered multiple times by various politicians or talk-show hosts in the course of a single day. Insist they stop to ponder that question before proffering a knee-jerk response. If they are aware enough to answer in the affirmative, you can point out that they aren't hearing original thoughts or observations, but merely a regurgitation of coordinated political talking points.

"As no one, especially at the dinner table, is fond of the sound of regurgitation, you may at long last be understood. Next time, with any luck, they won't even need you to remind them.

"It's been a pleasure...I think. Good night, and goodbye."

Dave makes his final exit from the radio station, wondering if his long dedication to spread truth has made any difference in the overall scheme of things. He begins to feel small, while the universe feels overwhelming.

Time to go get a drink.

57

MAGGIE RESIGNS

William Kohler sits at his desk, staring off into the ceiling tile. He appears deflated and confused, rare for someone of his stature and drive.

The door flies open without a knock. Maggie comes strolling into the office. The contrast between their moods is striking.

Maggie says, "You'll be amazed at what our research has turned up. This 'stand your ground' law allows people to get away with cold-blooded murder. The rate of legalized murders has skyrocketed. Yet in reviewing one case after another, we're concluding, without a doubt, almost none of those let off committed justifiable homicides. They avoided prosecution using this defense as an excuse. They weren't defending their lives, just their so-called ground. A finding of innocence doesn't mean a lack of guilt. The whole deal has gotten out of control. I think this story will open a lot of eyes, maybe even get this damn law repealed. I brought a stack of police reports that..."

Her esteemed editor puts his hand up, cutting her off. He is stone-faced. She looks surprised.

William says, "Our situation has changed."

"Changed? How?"

"Look, this needs to stop right now. We can't run the story."

Maggie is stunned. "What? Are you serious? Why?"

"The decision stands. It was made from above. They let me know, in no uncertain terms, if I didn't kill this story they'd bring in someone else to kill it. They've gone to the extraordinary length of getting a federal judge to file an injunction against our publishing it. My contract is up in two months. They could not only fire me tomorrow, but also prosecute me. I'm without leverage at this point."

"Why can't you fight this? You always stood up for what you believe. How can they get away with this?"

"Maggie, I'm sick about it, but there are big-money interests that won't let us print this. I don't own the newspaper; they do. We're up against a major confluence of corporate power. They're banded together. If you attack one of them, in this case the bottom line of the firearms industry, then you attack all of them. Some of our biggest sponsors will walk in solidarity. It's UCON. They run the show. We can't do a damn thing about it."

"Can't we? This is where we need to focus. Why don't we expose what this organization is doing to the country?"

"If you write about the inner workings of UCON, you'd better get the story published in the local *Free Times*, because you won't be working here anymore."

Maggie can't contain her anger. "They don't have that kind of power! Nobody has that kind of power!"

"One would think so. However, these bastards now own the United States Congress. They make them pass laws that won't even allow anyone to gather or publish records of gun crimes from a national data base."

"That's impossible. There's still the First Amendment. They can't stop us from speaking the truth to the people."

"Well, for starters, your friend within the Justice Department gave you information that was to be kept from the public. She could face federal prosecution under conspiracy charges if we were to publish this. Hell, in the state of Florida, they can even arrest a doctor for asking a patient if they have a firearm in the house. This shows the power of the gun lobby."

"What about the clandestine meeting with Senator Underwood? I've got our assets in place. This should be huge."

"Forget it. They've called it off. If any money is to change hands, it will happen at a different time and a different locale, and we won't be getting any record of it. I should also mention that the senator fired your friend."

As he delivers the shocking news, William slips Maggie a piece of paper, upon which he's written, "They've bugged my office."

She's stunned. When people refer to an Orwellian future, it's used as a colorful and overblown way of making a point. She can't comprehend that this is real. She's even half expecting a camera crew to come bursting in at any moment, claiming the whole scene was staged for a new reality TV show. However, it sinks in that although this may not be a show, it has become reality.

"Then so be it! If you don't have the guts to walk, I'll do it for you. I resign."

Maggie gets up and storms out of the room, leaving her job behind, carrying nothing out the door but her dignity.

58

JOE MEETS BERNARD

It's the noon hour, and the sidewalks are full of pedestrians. Due to cool weather, most are dressed in jackets or overcoats.

The whole point of wearing camouflage is to blend in. However, in the middle of town, anyone who wears such an outfit would accomplish the exact opposite by standing out. If one wanted to intimidate others in such an urban setting, or at least put them on their guard, it would also be the clothing of choice. This might explain why Joe Stupnik walks down a city street on this day, sporting this fashion.

Lawrence Peters is walking toward him, looking more urbane in an expensive leather coat. As these two gentlemen approach each other, they make eye contact. The closer they get, the more suspicious they become. As the distance between them closes, they lock in a stone-cold stare, coiled in expectation.

Passing each other, they brush shoulders. Perhaps both can share responsibility for the action. This kind of thing happens in high school hallways across the country. However, this isn't high school. This is the real world. They stop and turn around, squaring off. Neither speaks a word, but the vibe has turned hostile. They each wait for the other to make a move.

Both of them are moving their hands toward the inside of their jackets. The look turns from nervous suspicion to fear on both of their faces.

They draw their handguns, pointing them at each other. Both fire their weapons, squeezing the trigger multiple times. They shoot not only each other but also innocent bystanders. Six people fall to the ground, surrounded by others who are screaming and ducking for cover.

59

AT THE HOSPITAL

Lenny Rice has been on the police force for over thirty years, working up the ranks from traffic cop all the way to lieutenant. Through these decades of service, he has seen more than his share of irresponsible gunplay. In fact, he's rarely heard of someone using a gun for its stated purpose of self-defense. Only twice over his career has he investigated a murder case in which a prosecutor refused to seek charges. In these instances, there was a lack of substantial incriminating evidence, thus the shootings were ruled legal. In one instance, his gut told him the perpetrator was guilty as hell, only lucky enough to get away with it. In the other situation, there was a slight chance the suspect may have had legitimate grounds. Still, details were sketchy. However, since they passed the 'stand your ground' law in his state, Lenny has noticed a jump in unprosecuted street killings. In every incident, he has found the claim of self-defense to be as phony as a three-dollar lawyer. They haven't legalized the reasons for these murders, just the excuses.

As part of an ever-growing group of victims of gun violence, Lenny has also been touched by personal tragedy, as his wife was murdered by gunfire two years earlier. She had been having lunch at a downtown restaurant with a recently divorced friend. The ex-husband of her friend contested the divorce by showing up with a handgun, murdering his ex and Lenny's wife as they sipped their post-meal lattes.

It's always the same. Some deranged individual with a gun feels empowered to work out his differences with others in the worst way possible. That so many people would find a gun to be an instrument of self-defense is something Lenny has found to be laughable, if not so downright tragic. He sees quite the contrary in his line of work.

This afternoon would be no exception, as he receives a call about a street shooting in a downtown shopping district during the lunch hour. He drives straight to the hospital, where they've taken the victims along with the perpetrators.

Their latest adventure has landed both Joe Stupnik and Lawrence Peters in separate rooms of the emergency section. Both are under police guard. Detective Roger Dailey is questioning Joe while Lawrence is being questioned by Detective Steven Kotts. It's hard to determine which detective has drawn the short straw.

Roger grabs the TV remote and switches off the news, which has been showing a nonstop report on the shootout of the day. This startles Joe, who has been lying in bed, admiring the aftermath of his handiwork.

"Mr. Stupnik, do you know you shot three people? One's dead, one's in a coma, and another lies wounded in the next room."

Joe is coming out of a painkiller-induced fog. "Which one's in the next room, the black guy?"

"Yeah, the black guy."

"Well, he's the one I was shooting at. He was holding a gun and pointing it at me. I had to defend myself."

"That's interesting, because he says *you* were the one pointing a gun at *him*. He says he shot you in self-defense. One of you is lying. Who am I supposed to believe?"

As usual, Joe accepts no responsibility for his actions.

"I'm telling the truth. What would you do if some black guy was pointing a gun at you? What should I do, let him shoot me?"

Roger doesn't respond to the question. He's not the one being interrogated. "I've been looking at your record. It's funny how situations like this keep happening to you. Why is that?"

"I guess I'm just lucky," Joe says, smirking.

The detective can't resist the temptation to button up this case on the spot. He tries to be clever, coming up short. "Tell you what. Between you and me, I know it was you that drew first. I have a dozen witnesses who made that claim. If you'll agree to that and spare us the hassle of a trial, I think I can get the judge to let you off with a light sentence."

Joe isn't in too big of a fog to see through this lame approach. "How about you going into my wallet, which I'm sure you've already done, and handing me the business card of my attorney? My arm's a little sore, so will you dial his number for me, too?"

Roger sees he's getting nowhere with this guy. Without further comment, he leaves the room and goes to speak with his supervisor, Lieutenant Rice, who has been waiting out in the hallway. Lenny suspects he has got a real mess on his hands. Each gunman is blaming it on the other one. He was sure once the state handed out concealed-carry permits like bubblegum this would be the inevitable result. Who needs criminals when law-abiding citizens can now shoot *each other* as well?

Lenny asks Roger, "What do the witnesses say?"

Roger tells him what he was expecting to hear. "Oh, I've gotten about as many stories as there are onlookers. You know how these things go: everything happens so fast, people panic, duck for cover. It's hard to get a believable answer out of anybody."

"Keep trying. There's a real media circus here. We have six victims shot, two dead, one in a coma, and another clinging to life with a brain injury."

Detective Kotts walks up to join them. With lowered expectations, Lenny wants to find out what Lawrence Peters had to say. "What have you got?"

"I've gotten the same story. He's claiming he was shooting in self-defense, that this guy Stupnik was pointing a gun at him."

This exasperates Lenny. "They're both making the same claim, for God's sake!"

Steven doesn't put him at ease. "Lenny, I should tell you: both guys might end up walking."

Lenny is adamant. "We can't let that happen. This isn't the Wild West."

"Well, I'm afraid it is now."

Roger can only muse about it. "Too bad we couldn't find a joint on one of them. We could have at least locked somebody up for something. According to the 'stand your ground' law, these guys aren't even liable for any collateral damage."

Steven adds, "Yeah, but you know there will be a shit-load of lawyers on this looking to sue someone, maybe us!"

Lenny is unable to hide his disgust. "Cut 'em loose."

"Which one?"

"Both of them, goddamn it!"

He storms off, leaving the detectives to deliver welcome news to the two perpetrators. Meanwhile, a ravenous gaggle of attorneys is now flying overhead, circling this carcass of justice.

Lenny long predicted this kind of scenario. He was part of a select group of police officers called to testify before state lawmakers as they debated the ramifications of the 'stand your ground' law. Due to the political makeup of both chambers, it passed decisively. The script was provided to them by UCON, the true authors of the statute. Money, threats, and influence can always be counted on to trump common sense.

In his appearance before the state senate committee, Lenny had tried to describe real-world situations. Unfortunately, his audience of right-wing lawmakers has little to do with the real world, as it is a place they seldom venture. In their feeble minds, the armed good guy always triumphs over the armed bad guy, just like on television. The act of watching television is also the closest they'll ever get to reality. It's no wonder they form their opinions and judgments based upon whatever passes for popular entertainment.

Lenny had begged the lawmakers to reconsider. He had seen the negative results of too many concealed-carry permit holders looking to shoot first, think later. He could predict this 'stand your ground' nonsense adding one more excuse to shoot first without even having to think later. From ample experience, Lenny has learned that the last person whose word he could trust would be that of someone left holding a smoking gun. Now, this law would force him to accept their version of events. It's no longer an eye for an eye or an eye for a tooth. They've turned it into an eye for a hangnail.

60

THE VERDICT

The courthouse where the trial of Randy Steele has been taking place is now under siege by the national media, which has taken a major interest in this case. The street outside is full of satellite trucks. Reporters carrying microphones are scurrying about with cameramen in tow, positioning themselves for the nicest backdrop. The biggest networks have their own well-lit stages set up so their star correspondents can sit high above the crowd, looking as good as possible. Proper lighting is important. In television land, looks are number one, content is secondary.

The jury is through with their deliberations in record time. Normally, a swift decision would be a bad sign for the defense. Of course, there's nothing normal about this trial.

Judge Joseph T. Corcoran quiets the courtroom, which is overflowing with spectators, along with local and national media. He addresses the foreman. "Have you reached a verdict?"

"Yes, Your Honor. On the charge of manslaughter, we find the defendant not guilty."

The court, which is also full of uniformed police, erupts in anger. Randy hugs his attorney, then turns to sneer at the police sitting behind him. One officer tries to lunge at Randy, but the others hold him back.

Word spreads to the reporters stationed outside. One

correspondent is standing in front of the camera, broadcasting live to a national audience. "A near riot has broken out in Orlando, Florida. Randy Steele, charged in the murder of Patrolman Charles Morrison during a traffic stop, has been found not guilty."

The reporter spots a policeman walking by and shoves the microphone in his face. "Captain Nemeth, can you please tell me what you think of the verdict?"

The officer is in no mood for polite conversation. "This is outrageous! This case is an absolute travesty of justice! We should drug test the jury. First, this asinine 'stand your ground' rule lets citizens shoot each other for no reason, and now it even makes it OK to shoot a cop!"

The reporter persists, "What can you do about it?"

"I'd like to take the stupid son-of-a-bitch who wrote this law and…"

He realizes his comments are being beamed live to a national audience. "Never mind!"

He storms off.

61

MARILYN

The "Quad Killer," also known as MARILYN, is a weapon of the future, which is here now. It is an unmanned, low-altitude drone with its own one-hundred-round machine gun. One man can operate it with an iPad. He views everything by a front-mounted camera, controllable at a distance of up to a thousand yards. Although still in the prototype stage, it is fully operational. This device has become the latest flashpoint in the battle over gun control. That's because the gun lobby, along with its lackeys in Congress, is fighting to allow private citizens to possess this weapon.

Just imagine having your very own armed drone. Within the confines of your property, you can use it to spy on your neighbors and settle any disputes. If their dog should try to poop in your yard, you could catch it all on airborne video, along with Fido's demise at the flick of a button.

As Congress has made firearms off limits to any form of regulation, this latest and greatest gadget is being rushed to market in time for the Christmas holidays. As the industry is also now immune from any legal liability, a few misfires or explosive crashes here and there should do nothing to stop the rush to airborne death. It should be coming soon to a neighborhood near you, if not your own.

The MARYLIN drone will make a featured unveiling at the upcoming annual UGO convention. This act should really pack them in.

As the five-million-member organization has grown into an unstoppable financial juggernaut, it becomes accustomed to running roughshod over the three hundred and five million Americans who *don't* belong. Arms manufacturers, and millions of paranoid chumps who get suckered into forking over hard-earned funds as dues, line the deep pockets of this group. They're impervious to all challenges up to this point. They count on the whores and cowards in Congress to do their bidding, which means doing nothing, while the firearms industry rakes in mountains of cash. Money is money, and the bloodstains can be washed off.

62

THE CONVENTION

The UGO convention is taking place at the Raleigh, North Carolina, Exhibition Center. Many thousands are in attendance.

The crowd looks forward to the closing remarks on Sunday night. They have spent most of the last three days wandering through a thicket of exhibits showcasing the latest in weaponry. As is typical, people in attendance hear from several conflicted and confused speakers. One is there to sell them on arming up for personal protection. Another is there to convince them they need to arm up to repel the forces of the federal government, which are about to mass just outside their neighborhood. They believe federal troops are ready to swoop in at a moment's notice, all with the express purpose of confiscating the very guns that are supposed to ward them off. What's a paranoid half-wit to do: grab their gun and run to the window every time the sound of a distant helicopter reaches their inner sanctum?

They erect billboards outside the main hall, showcasing the public debut of the quad rotor drone killer, MARILYN. The crowd is excited, as their Republican servants in Congress fight to safeguard the right to own this thrilling new device, along with everything else in their arsenal. Hell, more than a few of the attendees possess enough firepower to wipe out George Washington's entire army, both before and after the Second Amendment was written.

It's time for the main event. Bill Fontaine takes the stage to deliver the keynote address, to be followed by an encore demonstration of MARILYN. He strides to the podium, knowing exactly what the people want, and is prepared to give it to them. His speech will be pure red meat, or rather pure venison for the crowd, many of which are dressed in hunting camouflage. A common trait of this audience is an intense dislike of government, with special emphasis on the left side of the aisle. The venom that flows forth comprises total vilification of Democrats, despite their having long capitulated to the gun lobby, whose power has now become dominant and absolute. In fact, one could say UGO is just another front for the Republican Party, if not vice versa.

The Democrats serve as an imaginary foil with which to galvanize the audience, most of whom would rather stand against something than for something. Having something to stand against proves to be a major money-raising device, both for UGO and the Republicans. Send us as much dough as possible, and we'll protect you from whatever straw man causes you the greatest fear, thus raising the greatest sum. Bill knows this, and he milks this cash cow for all its worth. He relishes his power and position, and isn't about to relinquish it to anyone or anything.

"Welcome to our annual gathering," he thunders. "Let's get straight to business. As you know, we're changing our focus to further protect our God-given right to self-defense. As we've finally succeeded in our arguments for states' rights regarding firearms, we now reverse course and push for stronger federal powers. They will then take precedence over the rights of states. This moves us one step closer to achieving our ultimate goal, which is to overturn all remaining firearm laws in the United States."

The crowd cheers. Though few of them ever bothered to read the Constitution, they believe our forefathers put the Second Amendment in place to guarantee the right to shoot whoever they like. Once the gun lobby takes over, they'll no longer even have to provide an excuse.

Bill continues. "As we've wielded tremendous power over state legislatures around the country, we shall now wield this power over the United States Congress."

More cheers from the crowd meet this line.

"We have the power and resources to eliminate any politician that stands in our way. Congress shall fear us. The president shall fear us. All those who seek to put restrictions on the right to bear arms shall fear us!"

The audience, now on its collective feet, roars at each utterance.

"We will make 'stand your ground' the law of the land!"

The throng continues to go wild.

"You have the birthright to defend yourself with deadly force wherever you are. It doesn't matter if you're in a hospital, a day care center, a courthouse, a shopping mall, or the class prom! The right to bear arms shall...not...be... infringed!"

Bill stands at the podium, beaming and soaking up the deafening sound of the roaring and cheering throng. The executive brain trust of the organization joins him onstage. They hold raised hands, taking bows for the people.

As they bask in the boisterous, overwhelming glory, behind them as planned, three MARILYN drones rise into the air. They are bathed by white, flashing strobes. The crowd roars even louder at this magnificent touch of showbiz.

The next step of the presentation underscores the untouchable audacity of UGO. At this moment, a large screen behind the stage lights up with a picture of Barack Obama. The armed drones are about to spin around by remote control and blow his image to smithereens.

63

DEVON TAKES AIM

Devon Richley, an inner-city youth of seventeen, sits at his laptop. Not your average kid, he excels at computer science. A full academic scholarship awaits him at Carnegie Mellon University.

Easily bored, as are many of his peers, Devon likes to spend his time competing in online video warfare games. Unbeknown to his parents, he's also an expert at infiltrating the computers of others. This is something he does for entertainment, not using his skills to disrupt anyone's e-commerce. He can leave Target's database to the Russians. One of his specialties is hacking gaming opponents, taking control of their video guns, and finessing his way to victory. All is fair in love and war.

On a quiet Sunday afternoon, Devon is searching for someone to hack. He soon discovers something interesting. In all his time spent participating in online warfare, he has never before seen such realistic imagery as that which now graces his monitor. Although not sure of what he has stumbled across, he finds a split video feed from three drones. A few keystrokes later, he's in control of them.

Despite being located two states away, Devon takes charge of the armed MARYLIN attack drones at the UGO convention, unaware that the reality he sees is anything but virtual. He's in command of them through a joystick, having overridden their previous controllers, who are now panicking backstage.

Through the live video feed to his laptop, Devon can see through their sights. He positions the controls to focus on the backs of some juicy-looking targets lined up on a stage. He hits a button, and all three drones open fire, sweeping across them.

With all the roaring and flashing lights, the audience doesn't realize at first what's taking place. It surprises them to watch their staged lineup of heroes suddenly jumping up and down, arms flailing. For several seconds, the leadership appears to be doing a crazy dance onstage. Many in the crowd think they are witnessing some maniacal celebration and are shocked by the outrageous gyrations coming from such a staid bunch. They respond by cheering even louder.

One after another, the leaders collapse to the floor. Bill Fontaine, the last one standing, is at center stage, performing a wild, macabre dance of death for several seconds more before collapsing.

The rapturous crowd has now caught on to what has happened, and the cheers turn into screams. Everyone is scrambling in fear for the exits. The MARILYN drones continue to fire, hitting many in the VIP seating area of the front rows. This section is filled with major contributors to the organization, along with owners and representatives of arms manufacturers. Their ranks are decimated in the carnage.

After running out of ammo, two of the drones fall to the convention floor. Devon manipulates the joystick control of the remaining craft to fly right out of the main entrance of the hall, chasing the fleeing members, shooting at their heels. After firing off every last round, he pilots the final drone to crash into a billboard outside displaying the proud UGO logo. Upon impact, the flying weapon explodes, burning up the smiling visage of the late Bill Fontaine.

Devon assumes this must be game over and awaits the posting of his final score. It's also game over for armed civilian drones, at least in the foreseeable future.

64

THE PUBLIC REACTION

In the days following the UGO massacre, public reaction is far different from that of every other mass killing that has preceded it. Instead of the solemn air expected to hover over such an occasion, the majority of Americans are positively giddy. Several news anchors can barely suppress a smile while delivering details of the affair to their audience. Many appear to be fighting the urge to crack up. Even the late-night television hosts, who usually respect a moratorium of indeterminate length after a big shooting, are soon making cracks about the fiasco. Jimmy Kimmel delivers a full fifteen-minute monologue devoted to the event. Stephen Colbert christens a new segment entitled "Stupid Gun Tricks."

While those at *Right-Wing News* wear black armbands and speak in solemn tones, other elements of the media are treating it more like the greatest entertainment in American history. In fact, the most upsetting information coming from this event is that a police dog outside the convention hall was injured in the resultant melee. Thousands donate to a fund set up for the canine. Millions from around the globe are cheered by the report a few days later from the supervising veterinarian that the dog, Peaches, is expected to make a full recovery.

The world finally has a laugh at the idiotic Americans and their guns. British newspapers are mocking the incident, running headlines such as "Live by the Sword, Die by the Sword."

A video of the event makes its way to YouTube. Bill Fontaine's extended dance of death, while being riddled with bullets, gets the slow-motion treatment. Someone scores a cartoonish music track to accompany the broadcast. It ends up getting the largest number of hits in YouTube history, displacing "Gangnam Style." Psy is crestfallen. The rest of the planet finds the whole thing hysterical. There's widespread abandonment of the atheism movement, as many adherents conclude there may be a God after all.

In a first for the modern era, UGO has been beaten back in its unending quest to gut all restrictions on firearms. The big push for personal drone protection, along with the effort to reintroduce fully automatic weapons, has been undermined, at least for now.

A brief press release is buried deep in the nation's newspapers. Jim Savage's upcoming Play 'Em and Slay 'Em Tour has been canceled, due to unspecified circumstances.

65

AT THE SUPERMARKET

Randy and Nancy Steele are rolling a shopping cart down the aisle of their local supermarket, the one outside which she met Maggie O'Rourke. Although most fellow shoppers don't give them a second look, some are quick to recognize Randy's scowling visage. He has been glowering through their TV screens for several weeks, first as a murder defendant, then as a plaintiff in lawsuits brought against the police, media, and everyone in sight. Being acquitted isn't enough. He aims to cash in, as he has become an overnight star in some circles.

Most people keep out of their way, although the Steeles engender more than their share of dirty looks. This seems fine to Randy, who has it in for humanity to begin with. When it comes to scowling, he can give as good as he gets, if not better. He enjoys being an intimidator. It keeps others out of his face, which is OK with him.

He intimidates no one more than Nancy, who dreams of having the courage to get as far away from him as possible. Even the simple act of putting the wrong loaf of bread into the shopping cart sets him off.

"Put that back! It costs too damn much!"

She meekly tries to defend her choice. "This bread is better for making sandwiches. It's whole grain. It's healthier."

Healthy eating doesn't make Randy's top-ten list of

concerns. "Fuck that. White bread is good enough."

"Don't you ever think about your health?"

"You should worry more about *your* health, bitch." He accompanies that line with a raised fist. "Put the goddamn bread back!"

Eager to assist, he grabs the loaf out of the cart and throws it to the floor. This draws exactly what they don't need: more scrutiny. A growing number of people are staring at the Steeles, who have managed once again to become the center of attention. He stares back at a lady who's glaring at him and shaking her head.

"What the fuck you looking at, bitch? You got a problem?"

A well-meaning elderly gentleman does the chivalrous thing, stepping forward. "Don't you talk that way to a woman."

While staring the man down, Randy reaches inside his jacket. "What the fuck are you gonna do about it?"

The man backs down.

Randy is becoming uncomfortable. "I don't like all these people looking at us."

Now it's Nancy who snaps. "Then you should quit making a scene. Why do you have to act so nasty to everyone? Is it because your father was mean to your mother?"

"Hey! You leave my father out of this. It's not his fault you're a stupid bitch. It's *your* goddamn fault. You never fucking listen. If I'm in a bad mood, it's because of you."

Maybe it's that they're out in public, gathering a crowd of spectators, but Nancy becomes emboldened. "Quit blaming everyone else for your problems! It's always somebody else's fault. You need to grow up."

He is not about to let her humiliate him in front of an audience. He slaps her. "I've had enough of your bullshit!"

He tries to grab her arm, but she pulls loose. "Come here, bitch!" He grabs her again.

She is becoming ever more defiant. "Let go of me."

He slaps her again and again, but she doesn't retreat.

Another female bystander steps up to the couple, focusing on Nancy. "You should walk away. Show some sense," she says.

Nancy replies, "The law says I don't have to."

With that, Nancy pulls a gun out of her purse and shoots Randy, right through the heart.

66

GOD HELP US

A bill to overturn the prohibition of felons, teenagers, and the insane to buy firearms is currently working its way through Congress.

God help us.